Round One

"You mean you're going to move the furniture around?" Deena sounded truly horrified.

"Yeah—why not? I mean, this room is fabulous, but it just needs a little work," Kathy said sincerely. "All we need to do is move both beds and desks over there"—she pointed to the far side of the room—"so we can use this space for dancing! And we'll put the speakers over here, against the wall, so they'll really *blast* out at us, no matter where we sit. Get it? Did I tell you that I was a singer in a rock band back home? Anyway, if I'm lucky, I'll meet some kids here and get into a band, and this would be a *perfect* place to rehearse! So what do you say?"

What could Deena say? She was completely stunned. Here was this person, this cousin she barely knew, tearing apart her masterpiece room, which she had slaved lovingly over for the past two days.

Cranberry Cousins
RIVAL ROOMMATES

BY CHRISTIE WELLS

A Troll Book

Acknowledgments

Many thanks to Suzanne Weyn for her work on developing the concept for *Cranberry Cousins*. And thanks to Megan Stine and H. William Stine, without whom this book could not have been written.

Library of Congress Cataloging-in-Publication Data

Wells, Christie.
    Rival roommates / by Christie Wells.
      p.   cm.—(The Cranberry cousins; #1)
    Summary: Fifteen-year-old Kathy, a lover of heavy metal music, outlandish clothes, and unorthodox behavior, suddenly finds herself sharing a bedroom with her more traditional, "perfect" cousin Deena, who takes it upon herself to correct and improve Kathy's lifestyle.
    ISBN 0-8167-1496-7 (lib. bdg.)   ISBN 0-8167-1497-5 (pbk.)
    [1. Cousins—Fiction.   2. Individuality—Fiction.] I. Title.
II. Series: Wells, Christie. Cranberry cousins; #1.
PZ7.W4635Ri 1989
[Fic]—dc19   88-16954

A TROLL BOOK, published by Troll Associates
Mahwah, NJ 07430

Chapter 1

"What if she hasn't changed?" Kathy Manelli asked. She was sitting in the passenger seat as her mother drove their dusty red van into the town of Cranford. She turned to her mother with a pleading look. "This whole thing will be a disaster if she hasn't changed."

Thirty-seven-year-old Nancy Manelli reached out and patted her daughter without taking her eyes off the road. "Of course she's changed," she said. "It's been four years. You've certainly changed in four years. And I'm sure she has, too. You're both fifteen now."

Kathy looked out the window at the trees, which were already turning a beautiful autumn gold, and caught a glimpse of herself in the right side mirror.

It was true, she *had* definitely changed since she was eleven. Her dark brown hair was cut all different layers. She wore it moussed and wavy and wild, so it looked as if she'd just been through an electrifying experience. Her big brown eyes, which used to look like puppy eyes, were now transformed into bullets by her dark eye make-up. And her iridescent fingernail polish sparkled against her knee-length black sweater, which she wore over black tights. To cap it all off, there was an oversized earring dangling from just one ear. That was the Kathy Manelli look. The kids at her old school either hated it—or loved it so much that they imitated it. But it was an unmistakable look, and everyone recognized it.

Sure, Kathy thought, running her fingers through the shortest part of her hair. Everything changes. The skylines change, the shorelines change, styles change, traffic lights change ... your address changes. Even when you don't want it to. So why shouldn't my cousin, Deena Scott, change?

"She's probably not bossy anymore," Kathy said hopefully. Then she thought about the last time they had seen each other, four years ago. Deena had gone through Kathy's dolls and picked out the ones Kathy should throw out, in an effort to organize her collection.

"And she probably got over being such a total know-it-all," Kathy said.

Know-it-all?! They must have invented the term the day Deena was born. At age ten Deena had selected her college and her major—and then she picked a school for Kathy, too.

Forget it, Kathy decided. This wasn't going to work out.

"I think I forgot something at home. Can we turn around and go back?" Kathy said.

"It's not home anymore and there's no reason to freak out," answered her mother. "Just go with the flow, Kath. It's been a long drive."

A long drive, for sure. All the way from the West Coast to New England—from San Francisco to Cranford, New Hampshire—in one week. One week. It was such a very short time to change your whole life.

Just a few weeks ago, Kathy, her mom, and her little brother, Johnny, had been living a typical single-parent life in California. Her mom had been working as a wait-ress in the evenings and writing poetry until dawn, while Kathy made macaroni and cheese for dinner more nights than not.

Then everything changed.

"We're getting out of here," Nancy told her kids one day, and abruptly began packing. "I've decided to go along with something my sister's been begging me to do all summer. We're going to go live in my grandparents' old country inn, in Cranford! Your aunt Lydia and I in-herited it last spring, and we've decided to open it up again. It's a wonderful, funky old place—very New Eng-land. You've never seen it, but I've loved it all my life. So get packed, because we've got to make it to the East Coast in time for you to start school."

And that was it. There wasn't time for "Mom, let's sit down and discuss this as three mature people." There

3

wasn't even time for "Mom, let's sit down and discuss this as one heartbroken, hysterical widow and two confused kids."

The next thing she knew, Kathy was watching the United States slide by as her mom aimed the van steadily east. And now, after seven dusty days and nights on the road, they were almost there.

Slowly Nancy Manelli wound her way through the quaint New England town, trying to remember the way without consulting a map.

At a stop light she sucked in her breath and held it a minute.

"What is it?" Kathy asked.

"I lied. I'm starting to freak out, too," Nancy admitted to her daughter.

"Too late for that, Mom," said Kathy.

The truth was, they were all feeling nervous—even nine-year-old Johnny in the back seat. However, Kathy was feeling excited, too. She was excited about living in an enormous old Victorian house, especially the way she imagined it. In her mind it was painted white, with rocking chairs and swings on the porch . . . and interesting guests heading for the beach in summer and for the ski slopes in winter.

And she was even secretly excited about living with her aunt Lydia and Deena. It would be nice to have a big family again. Sometimes they all got pretty lonely since Dad died.

If only she didn't have to share a room with Deena! But maybe her mom was right, and Deena had changed.

4

They might even have fun together. And having Deena around would definitely make it easier moving into a new town where she didn't know anyone. If only Deena had changed; she kept her fingers crossed.

* * *

At that very moment Deena Scott—blond, graceful, and pretty—was standing in a large sun-filled room on the third floor of the old Cranberry Inn, looking at her watch. She wondered how long it would be until Kathy arrived. But more importantly, she wondered what Kathy would be like. Would she be the same tough-talking, never-a-dull-moment, adventure-starved kid she'd been four years ago? Of course not—Deena knew that. In four years Deena was sure Kathy would have learned some manners and developed some grace. By now she must have grown up to be as sensitive, intelligent, and mature as Deena herself. After all, they were cousins, weren't they? Flesh and blood. It bound them together like the roots of an oak tree are bound to the soil, Deena thought; she made a mental note to write that down in her journal. It was a great line, and she'd probably want to use it in a story or poem some day.

Nervously she went about adding the finishing touches to the room she and Kathy would share. But the room was really complete already.

Deena had put vases of spectacular flowers and fall leaves on every available surface. She had tacked up her three favorite posters on the wall and arranged a friendly choir of stuffed animals on the window seat. And she had put her most prized possession—a baseball with Carl Yastrzemski's autograph—prominently on a shelf but out of the sunshine, so it wouldn't fade. Deena wasn't much of a baseball fan, but the ball had been her father's. When her parents got a divorce a few years ago, he gave it to Deena and promised he'd visit it at least once a month. He hadn't always kept that promise, but she kept the ball anyway, and treasured it because it had meant so much to her father.

Then Deena stood in the doorway of the bedroom and evaluated her work. Yes, it was definitely almost perfect. Of course, one side of the room was somewhat empty, because Deena had had to leave space for Kathy's things. But the other side—Deena's side—was like a picture-book drawing of every girl's fantasy room.

The wooden four-poster bed was covered with lacy pillow shams and a bedspread of small blue flowers. Deena's books were neatly arranged on shelves. The antique wooden desk was well organized with writing and studying materials, including a rainbow assortment of papers and pens. And there were two wonderful old chairs in the room—one a rocker and the other an overstuffed chair with a big flower-print slipcover.

It was the almost-perfect room—but not quite. And Deena knew its flaw. There was only one chest of drawers. If Kathy had as many sweaters as Deena, they'd have to stack them on the floor.

Deena went to her desk, took out a sheet of her stationery, and selected her favorite pen. *Wants and Ne-*

cessities, by Deena Scott, she wrote at the top of the page. *Additional drawer space*, she wrote. She looked around and noticed that her bottle of cream rinse was almost empty. Deena's shoulder-length blond hair tended to be dry, but she remembered that Kathy's was more oily. *Cream Rinse—normal*, she decided with a smile. *Telephone*, and underneath it she added, *two-line telephone or call waiting?*

Deena hoped this room would become home for Kathy and her. They would talk about the clubs they belonged to and the boys they liked, and the boys they hated. Maybe Kathy would even want to read her poetry. Maybe they could become lifelong friends. Deena hoped.

* * *

Nancy Manelli's red van was beginning to send up hostile smoke signals from the radiator.

"Hang tough, gang. We're almost there," she said with a tired smile. A few minutes later the van came to a stop in front of a large old neglected house. To Kathy, it looked like it would need a lot of work just to be called run-down. There was a sign out front which said:

Cranberry Inn
Come in for a warm welcome and a hot muffin.

"Well, there it is," Nancy Manelli announced, smiling. Kathy took a deep breath of crisp September air and stared at the three-story house. "It looks better from a distance," Kathy said. "Three thousand miles away!"

"It's been empty since Grandma and Grandpa Delaney died," Nancy said wistfully. "It just needs a little fixing up, that's all—and that's what we've come to do."

"Too bad we forgot to pack the bulldozer," Kathy said. Her mother shot her one of those quit-exaggerating looks, but Kathy couldn't help it. This was not exactly the charming old New England inn her mother had advertised—at least, not yet. And Kathy knew that "a little fixing up" meant there were major chores in her future.

Johnny, however, who had been uncharacteristically quiet until now, took one look at the house and shouted excitedly, "Grand Slam!" Recently Johnny had been describing everything in baseball terms—probably because he was counting down the weeks to the World Series.

Before Kathy could even get out of the way, Johnny pushed past her and was out of the van. He took the front steps two at a time and leaped onto the porch. Nancy followed closely behind.

Well, I guess I have to get out of the van sometime, Kathy thought. She checked her hair in the mirror to be sure it looked just right. She wanted to make a good first impression with the famous Kathy Manelli look.

Then she climbed out of the van and joined her mother on the porch.

Nancy opened the front door and Kathy looked in.

"Hey! Anyone here? You've got customers!" Nancy called as they walked into an empty open area with a cathedral ceiling. At one side was an enormous stone fireplace and sitting room. All the way across the room was a wide stairway that must lead to the two floors of guest rooms. In the middle of this large open space was a long wooden desk where guests could register.

"Nancy?" yelled a voice from somewhere in the dark interior.

Kathy's aunt, Lydia Delaney Scott, a tall, thin, pretty woman, came rushing in from the back of the house. She was older than Kathy's mother and more sophisticated. Instead of Nancy's long, brown hair, which hadn't been cut in a couple of years, Lydia's hair was frosted blond and very stylish. While Nancy wore blue jeans and a tie-dyed shirt she had owned in the sixties, Lydia's designer jeans and multi-colored, hand-knit bulky sweater were the latest fashion.

"I can't believe you're really here," Lydia said, hugging her sister tightly. "It's been so long since I've seen you!"

"When did you and Deena get here?" Nancy asked, wiping a sentimental tear from her cheek.

"Two days ago," Lydia answered. She gave Johnny and Kathy a quick hug. But Kathy noticed the sidelong glance she gave her. "We're almost moved in," she said, kissing Johnny on the cheek.

"Foul ball," Johnny said, wiping the kiss off his face. Then he added, "I'm thirsty, Mom," in his what-have-you-done-for-me-lately voice.

"How about a glass of the official drink around here? Cranberry juice!" Aunt Lydia offered.

"A swing and a miss," Johnny said.

"Pardon me?" asked Lydia.

"He doesn't like cranberry juice," Kathy translated.

"Chocolate milk?" Lydia said.

"Holy cow! It's a home run!" shouted Johnny.

"Where's Deena?" Nancy asked.

"Deena! They're here!" Lydia called.

All eyes moved to the stairway at one end of the room where Deena suddenly appeared. She stood looking down and brushing her silky, shoulder-length blond hair.

"Hi, you guys," she called, starting down the wide wooden stairway. But halfway down she stopped, frozen from the surprise of seeing—really seeing—Kathy for the first time in four years.

Both girls had secretly hoped that meeting the other would be like meeting a soulmate. Now that the moment of truth had arrived, neither one was prepared for it. In fact, the truth hurt.

"Hi," Kathy said.

"Hi," Deena said, looking like a statue of a girl with a brush stuck in her hair. Finally she took her arm down.

"So, uh . . . " Deena stumbled around. "How was your odyssey?"

"Odyssey??"

"You know—your trip cross-country," Deena said. "It must have been great for you. Like one of those adventures you were always planning when we were kids."

"Yeah, well, I liked sagebrush and road dirt a lot more when I was younger," Kathy said. "I've changed."

"I can see that," Deena said. "I mean, you've changed a *lot*."

"What did you expect?" Kathy said, laughing. "Puberty gets to the West Coast, too, you know—just three hours later."

"It's just that the last time I saw you, I mean you used to be, well, really, when did you start looking like ... "

Deena stood there starting one sentence and then another and not finishing any of them. But Kathy thought she knew what word Deena was looking for: *weird*.

"Well, anyway," Deena said, changing the subject, "I went down to the square in Cranford this morning to check things out. The guys are O.K.-looking, but they're definitely running at least eight months behind on maturity levels. So you might want to go a little more subtle with the hair and jewelry."

She was starting already! Kathy let out an audible sigh but held her tongue.

"No, honestly," Deena went on in a confidential voice. "We won't get anywhere scaring them."

"The scared ones aren't worth chasing," Kathy said.

"Still sarcastic," Deena said, tightening her smile a notch.

"And you're still telling me what to do," Kathy said.

They were having one of those awkward moments, which both girls had a feeling wasn't going to be unusual in their future.

"Well, the Cranberry Inn is all ours now," Lydia said, breaking the tension. "And I'll bet you're dying to see your room, aren't you, Kathy?"

"Yeah, as a matter of fact, I am," Kathy said. Then she

gave Deena a genuine smile and added, "Come on, Deena. You and I never did get along all that well, so it's going to take time. But this'll work out."

Deena's face relaxed, too. "Yeah—it'll work out," she said. But for once in her life, Deena Scott didn't sound absolutely, positively sure.

Chapter 2

The stairs leading to the third floor were lined with delicate spindles, and the stairways twisted and turned three times. At the first landing Kathy glanced down the hallway and saw a group of guest rooms. Even from where she stood, she could tell that they were a mess of cobwebs, old furniture, and dust.

But about halfway up the next staircase, the dust disappeared and the wooden stairs took on a waxy gleam. Kathy smiled appreciatively. Deena had already left her mark.

Finally, on the third floor, they walked into a large, irregularly shaped space. And Kathy saw the room that was going to be hers—Deena's and hers, she reminded herself—from now on.

The room *was* special, and Kathy loved it instantly, although she immediately saw ten things that needed to be changed.

It was a very large and sunny room with high, slanting ceilings and windows on three sides. The front window bowed out facing the street and was lined with a window seat piled high with stuffed animals. In the corner there was a turret, which made a small round area. It, too, had a window seat with tiny flowered cushions on it.

"I've tried to establish a theme of contemporary country living," Deena explained.

Kathy looked at the posters of baby animals and the poster called Wildflowers of the Northeast—and couldn't help wondering *what* country Deena was talking about!

But she didn't say it. Instead, she sat down on the empty bed, which creaked instead of bounced. Kathy frowned.

"Oh, well," she said, "this bed will give me a good excuse to miss school."

"Huh?" Deena said.

"Backaches," Kathy explained. She made a funny face, as if faking agonizing pain, and then laughed. Then she noticed Deena's list of Wants and Necessities and started reading it.

"That's private," Deena said, snatching the list away. "Do you want to trade beds?"

"No, don't worry. I'll just move mine over to a window," Kathy said. Even though you *did* take the best window, she thought to herself. But she didn't say it.

14

"You mean you're going to move the furniture around?" Deena sounded truly horrified.

"Yeah—why not? I mean, this room is fabulous, but it just needs a little work," Kathy said sincerely. "All we need to do is move both beds and desks over there"—she pointed to the far side of the room—"so we can use this space for dancing! And we'll put the speakers over here, against the wall, so they'll really *blast* out at us, no matter where we sit. Get it? Did I tell you that I was a singer in a rock band back home? Anyway, if I'm lucky, I'll meet some kids here and get into a band, and this would be a *perfect* place to rehearse! So what do you say?"

What could Deena say? She was completely stunned. Here was this person, this cousin she barely knew, tearing apart her masterpiece room, which she had slaved lovingly over for the past two days.

"I want my desk where it is," Deena finally said in her most controlled tone of voice. "I'll need the best light to study."

"Study?" Kathy said.

"Yes, study. You know, read books, underline books, read notes, underline notes, solve problems, underline solutions," Deena said. "Don't tell me you don't study."

"O.K., I won't tell you," Kathy said with a laugh. She picked up her purse and started rummaging around, looking for something.

"If you don't study," Deena said slowly, "how do you get good grades?"

"I listen, I get around, and I think," Kathy said. Finally Kathy found what she was looking for. She pulled a small

15

atomizer of room scent out of her purse and sprayed it into the air. It was musk.

"There. Now this place smells like home."

Deena almost choked, but she swallowed quickly and said, "Right. That's what you ought to do. Personalize this room. Really make it yours."

"Thanks. I'm glad I have your permission. In fact, I think I'll go down and get some of my stuff out of the van now." Kathy tossed her hair as she left the room.

Deena sat on her own bed, hugging her knees, and tried to maintain her composure. Same old Kathy, she thought to herself. Sweet as candy apples one minute and tough as nails the next. She's just trying to unnerve me. Unfortunately, there aren't many people in the free world who are better at it than Kathy Manelli! But two can play at that game—and I'm not going to let her win.

A few minutes later Kathy was back with an armload of clothes, boxes, and bags.

Deena watched as her cousin unpacked, dropping clothes in piles on the floor according to color.

"You want to hear something?" Kathy asked, pulling a cassette from a box. "It's my favorite band. Nuclear Waste. I've got all their tapes. I don't suppose you're into heavy metal?"

"Hardly," Deena said.

"Don't worry. A couple of weeks of my tapes and you'll be a certified head banger," Kathy said.

"I don't doubt it," Deena said. At that moment she knew what she wanted more than anything on her list of

Wants and Necessities, and she wrote it down: HEADPHONES!

Kathy dug around in another box and whipped out an enormous Nuclear Waste poster. "Hey, look, could you get crazy just looking at them?" she said.

Deena looked, but she didn't know what to say. It was an overwhelming poster. It looked like it was taken exactly two seconds before the four snarling, sneering musicians in black leather destroyed the hotel room they were in. They probably mangled the photographer, too.

"I know the perfect place for this," Kathy said.

Deena held her breath and envisioned the poster in *her own* idea of the perfect place: folded up on the bottom of a cat box. Putting it on the back of the only door to the room was the worst place she could think of.

"Don't put that there!" Deena blurted out as Kathy taped it to the door. "It's on my side of the room!"

Suddenly there were footsteps on the landing. Then Nancy, Kathy's mother, stuck her head in the room.

"How's it going?" she asked.

"Oh, hi," Deena said calmly. "Maybe you can help us avert a small disagreement. Kathy wants to put that poster up *on the door!* But the door is on my side of the room. I'll see *them* every time I go out."

"Hey, I've got a window on my side of the room," Kathy said. "Feel free to use it for going out anytime you want."

Deena scrunched up her mouth just the way her mother always did.

17

"Mellow out, Kathy," Nancy said. "Don't make such a fuss over one little rock poster. Deena has to have a chance to make this room hers, too, you know. And there's only one door, so you can't claim it all to yourself."

"Thanks, Aunt Nancy!" Deena said, beaming. But she wasn't too thrilled when she saw the scowl on Kathy's face.

Just as her daughter had done, Nancy Manelli picked up Deena's list and started reading it. She saw *additional drawer space* written there. "You know, I just saw a great old dresser in the garage," Nancy said. "It's got to be stripped and refinished, but it would give you guys some more drawers."

"We could definitely use some more drawers," Deena said to Kathy. "You need to put your clothes away."

Kathy looked at the piles of clothes on the floor.

"I *have* put my clothes away," she said.

Deena looked alarmed.

"Very funny, Kath," Nancy said. "But I don't think Deena got your joke."

"Don't worry. She's getting all of them, Mom!" Kathy said.

Nancy ran her hand through her hair to lift it away from her temples and gazed around the room. Then she came to the point of her visit.

"Kath—how'd you like to give me a hand? Your brother won't come out of his room. He says the door got locked, and he doesn't know how to unlock it. He wants to talk to you."

"Sure thing," Kathy said, following her mom down the stairs.

Deena followed right along behind Kathy.

"He's nine years old and he doesn't know how to unlock a door?" Deena said.

"The locks he knows how to unlock are three thousand miles away, O.K.?" Kathy snapped. Dust bunnies were scampering out of her way as she walked quickly down the hall to Johnny's room.

"Oh, you mean he's feeling tense because he's in a new environment," Deena said. "Don't worry—I know how to handle this."

"So do I," Kathy said. "What are you going to do? Fill out his college application for him?"

"You *would* remember that," Deena said through tight lips.

"Johnny," Kathy called, knocking on her brother's door.

"Hey, Johnny, this is your cousin, Deena."

Kathy shot Deena a serious warning look.

"Double header," Johnny said without much enthusiasm from inside his room.

"Johnny," Deena said, trying to ignore Kathy's glare, "you've got to come out of there."

"I can't," Johnny said.

"I know," Kathy said. "Johnny—"

But Deena interrupted again. "Come on, Johnny. You've got to come out. Because there's something really great and you've got to see it."

19

"What?" asked Johnny.

"I don't believe this," Kathy said, fuming. She narrowed her eyes into slits, but Deena ignored her.

"Kittens," Deena said. "Brand-new kittens."

"Really?" Johnny said, showing signs of life. "What color?"

"Don't lie to him!" Kathy said when she heard Deena mention kittens. "Boy, you sure don't know much about kids."

"I'm *not* lying," Deena insisted. "There really are kittens. Two tigers, one black, and two calico," she called through the door to Johnny.

"What a line-up," Johnny said.

Deena gave Kathy a nod and a smile and whispered, "Psychology." Then she spoke up again.

"They're only about three weeks old. I found them in the attic when I got here. But they need someone to give them names. Don't you want to see them?"

"Sure," Johnny said. There was a pause. "Slide them under the door."

Deena's eyes snapped open wide. "Johnny, you come out of there right now!"

"I can't."

"You're out on strikes," Kathy announced to her cousin triumphantly. Then she moved into position nearest the door. "Hey, Johnny, you don't have to come out. It's O.K. How about me coming in?"

During the pause, Kathy looked at Deena's scrunched-up mouth. "It's going to stick like that one of these days," she whispered.

The doorknob rattled and turned, and then the door opened a crack. Kathy opened the crack just wide enough to fit through, but Deena slipped in behind her before Kathy could slam the door.

The sun was going down and the room was turning from gray to black. Johnny had retreated to sitting on the floor in front of his unmade bed.

"How about some light in here?" Kathy asked.

"The lamps don't work," Johnny said.

"You don't have any light bulbs," Kathy noticed.

"They probably don't sell them here," Johnny said.

"There are flashlights in a box. I packed them," Kathy said.

"You did?" Deena said almost admiringly.

It was almost too dark to read the labels on the boxes stacked in Johnny's room. But Kathy finally found one marked FLASHLIGHTS. She snapped on four of them and stood them in the corners around the room. Dim light and big ceiling shadows—it felt a little like camping in the wilds.

"It's a good room," Kathy said. "Bigger than the one you had."

"It's too big," Johnny said. "And it's on the first floor. You're all the way on the third floor. You'll be up there all the time."

Kathy sat down on the bed and pulled Johnny up next to her. She put her arm around him. "Hey—you can come up anytime you want," Kathy said.

"Of course, you'll have to remember to knock first," Deena added quickly.

"Deena!" Kathy said, as though words could strangle someone. "Isn't your mother calling you? Or your destiny? Or an army recruiter?"

"Sorry," Deena said. Then she came over and sat down on the bed on the other side of Johnny. "You know, I've never lived with a little brother *or* a roommate before," Deena said. "But you know what I think? I think we're all going to be friends here, Johnny. And all kinds of people are going to come here, maybe famous people, and stay in the inn. We'll get to know what they're like and what they think about life. This is going to be a rare and exciting learning experience."

Kathy looked at her cousin and didn't know whether to hug her, burst out laughing, or just gag.

"Time out. I'm starving," Johnny said.

Deena and Kathy both laughed.

"Well, come on out and we'll get some dinner going," Kathy said.

"Can't you bring me something?" Johnny asked.

"Aren't you coming out?" Deena said.

"Well, I gotta unpack my boxes, don't I?" Johnny said.

"Yeah, of course," Kathy said. "Want some help?"

"Sure," Johnny said. "But I want *both* of you to help me."

Deena and Kathy looked at each other for a moment. The flashlights sparkled on Kathy's earring and Deena's soft hair. Finally Deena spoke.

"Sure, we'll help you unpack," she said brightly. "In fact, I know just exactly how you should arrange your room!"

Chapter 3

The next day began early. Too early for Kathy. She didn't want to get up in the first place, and especially not when she heard what her aunt Lydia had planned. It was an endless list of projects for everyone, and each one began with the words *clean up*. This was not Kathy's prime idea of how to spend her first day in her new home.

"I'm going out, Mom!" Kathy yelled, standing by the front door. "Do you need anything?"

"Yes! Help!" her mother answered from the attic.

"First thing when I get back," Kathy called. She was almost out the door when Deena appeared on the landing.

"Where are you going?" Deena asked.

"Just to look around town," Kathy said. "Gotta pick up some stuff."

"I could save you loads of time. I know where everything is in town," Deena said.

Who was trying to save time? Certainly not Kathy. In fact, she didn't care if it took her all day to get back.

"I'll come with you. It's no trouble," Deena said before Kathy could answer. "I've just got to change my clothes, dry my hair, make a list, and put on my make-up."

"I'd like to get there before dark," Kathy said.

Deena scrunched her mouth, but she ran up to the third floor to get ready without saying anything.

It was a beautiful fall day despite the fact that Deena kept calling it the "quintessential autumn morning." As the two cousins walked to the village, the bite of the air, the brilliant colors, and the crunch of the fallen leaves were all new to Kathy. And she had to admit that it was better than fall in San Francisco, which consisted mostly of fog.

When they got to the village, they did some window shopping first.

"Couldn't you just die?" Deena said, raving about a cashmere sweater with a hood.

It was all one color. It had no feathers on it. It was waist-length instead of knee-length. Kathy could barely keep awake just looking at it.

But then Kathy saw a bike shop, and she quickly went in to buy a bike lock and chain.

"I didn't know you had a bike," Deena said.

Kathy just rolled her eyes and wrapped the chain

around her waist and locked it. "I needed a new belt," she explained.

They walked past an ice-cream shop, which was filled with high school kids hanging out. Most of them were wearing ski vests or bright bulky sweaters.

"Let's go," Kathy said as they looked in the shop through the plate-glass window. "No one's in there."

"No one?" Deena said. "You must be getting refracted glare from the sun. Kathy, the place is packed. This can only be described as an optimum moment for meeting our classmates."

"Forget it," Kathy said, walking away. "I'm not interested in just taking a body count."

"O.K.," Deena said. "But there is one place I want to go, and you have to come with me." She started dragging Kathy toward a building with a sign that said Cranford Board of Education over the door.

"What are we doing here?" Kathy said as they walked down the bright fluorescent-lighted hallway. "I feel like I'm turning myself in for a crime I didn't commit."

"This will only take a second," Deena said. "I have to ask them a very important question."

Deena pulled open the door and walked into the main office.

"Hello, I'm Deena Scott and this is Kathy Manelli," Deena said to the woman in charge. "We're transfer students at your high school this fall."

Kathy cringed. Why does she have to sound like she's running for class president?

"Yes, I know," said the woman. "Your mothers already registered you by mail. How may I help you?"

"We were wondering why we haven't received our class schedules yet," Deena said.

Kathy gave Deena a what-do-you-mean-*we* look.

"You'll get your schedules on the first day of class. I'm afraid our new computer system wasn't installed in time to mail them out," the woman said in a friendly voice. "But I must say, it's wonderful to see two students who are so responsible and concerned. I'm sure both of you girls will be very happy at Cranford High."

Kathy rolled her eyes again and thought, How can I possibly wait another three days until I get my schedule? I'll probably die waiting. Just don't wake me.

* * *

Three days later Deena woke up before the birds. She hopped out of bed onto the cold hardwood floor. But she didn't make a sound, thanks to years of ballet lessons. Then she tippy-toed to the closet to pick out something to wear. It was the first day of school, and she wanted to look absolutely perfect. But more than that, she wanted Kathy to look . . . well . . . forget absolutely perfect. How about just normal? Kathy wouldn't mind a little help coordinating her clothes for the first day of school, would she?

She opened Kathy's closet door and cringed. It was going to be tough finding something for Kathy to wear. She moved Kathy's clothes around until finally she found a combination she almost liked. Deena put them in the middle of the rack and pushed everything else to the back, so Kathy would see these clothes first.

Then Deena began doing her wake-up exercises. "Time to get up," she called to Kathy, alternating between touching her toes and doing side stretches.

"Deena, it's six-thirty in the morning. I sleep late." Deena watched Kathy's face disappear under her pillow.

"Don't go back to sleep now," Deena said, "or your face will be puffy when you get to school."

"I'll sign in as Poppin' Fresh, O.K.?" Kathy mumbled.

Deena went through her own closet, matching her clothes with the morning light. But she just couldn't stand to see Kathy sleeping in. "Well, when *are* you getting up? You don't want to be late."

"Why?"

"Why?" Deena sat down on the edge of Kathy's bed. "Because it's the first day of school, that's why! Because it's the start of a whole new and exciting life! And because today's the day every student will check you out, look you over, evaluate you, and give you a grade. And that grade sticks. We've got to be our best today."

"You can handle that for both of us, can't you?" Kathy said.

Deena rolled her eyes and checked the clock. No point in arguing. If there was one thing Deena knew about her cousin, it was that Kathy Manelli could not be talked into anything. The more you tried to persuade her, the harder she'd fight.

So Deena plunged into her morning routine: showering, blow drying her hair, eating breakfast, and checking on the kittens in the attic. When she got back, Kathy was still sleeping. Deena dressed quickly, nudged her cousin one more time, and then left for school.

Cranford High School was only a twenty-minute walk away. But today it seemed like twenty miles. Deena could hardly wait to get there, to really and truly start her new life. This was it—*this* was where her whole life for the next three years would really take shape. She hoped it wasn't that different from her old school in Boston.

Even before Deena saw the old stone school building, she heard its tall Roman numeral clock chime in the tower. She hoped it was loud enough to wake Kathy up!

The narrow halls of the high school were dark and noisy as Deena entered. And the kids all obviously knew one another. For a moment Deena felt like a complete outsider.

But then she remembered something one of her teachers in Boston once told her. "A stranger is just someone you don't know." It was probably the dumbest thing anyone ever said to her, and thinking of it now suddenly made her laugh.

"Nice laugh," said a tall, blond guy who smiled as he walked past her. He had "upperclassman" written all over him.

"Thanks!" Deena called to him. "How do I find my homeroom?"

He stopped, turned, and looked at her with his arms

28

crossed, still smiling. "New student, huh? Senior? Junior?" he asked.

"Sophomore," Deena said with a smile. She could tell he was surprised.

"Check the lists outside the main office," he said. "And pray you don't have Mr. Millander."

"Thanks," Deena said.

So far her day was off to a good start. She had already talked to a great guy! Deena quickly found the office and spotted her name on the list. She was in Mrs. Friedman's homeroom class.

A blond girl standing next to Deena looked at her and moaned. "I got Mr. Millander," she said. She had a pretty face that was very thin.

Deena shook her head sympathetically as if she really knew who Mr. Millander was and why no one would want to be in his class.

"What do you think I should do? Change my name?" the girl asked.

Deena didn't know the girl or the teacher, but she knew a plea for advice when she heard one.

"Give him a smile and ask him how his summer was," Deena said.

"It's so simple, it just might work," the girl said with a laugh. "Thanks. I'm Jessie Martin."

"Deena Scott."

"You're new, aren't you?"

"Yes, but I was hoping it didn't show. How did you know?" Deena said.

"If you were here last year, I'd remember you," Jessie said, smiling.

"Thanks," Deena said. She knew that was a compliment.

"Come on. You'd better hurry. The bell's going to ring," Jessie said. "Hey, maybe we'll be in some classes together. Or I'll see you in the cafeteria," she called as she walked away.

Deena found Room 203, Mrs. Friedman's class, and looked in.

Well, this is it, she told herself. The big first impression. Everyone's going to be watching, so remember: be graceful, be friendly, and check your seat for tacks before you sit down. Sophomore boys may still think that's funny.

Deena walked into the classroom and sat down right in the middle of the front row.

When the bell rang, Mrs. Friedman, a young woman with large dark eyes and long black hair, stood up from her desk. "Good morning, everyone," she said. "As you all know, the computer system was down until a few days ago. So you didn't get your schedules in the mail. But don't worry. I'm going to pass them out to you right away and end the suspense. Shelley Agar? Kim Ashwer?"

Mrs. Friedman walked up and down the aisles handing out computer printout schedules. Meanwhile, Deena looked around the room, making eye contact with all the new and unfamiliar faces.

Wait a minute—that wasn't an unfamiliar face at all!

Deena stared at the person sitting all by herself, in the

30

last seat in the back of the room. It was Kathy! And she wasn't wearing the clothes Deena had picked out. Deena felt a small shock go through her. Of course she knew Kathy was going to the same school, but who expected to see her in the same classroom? Was she going to make some cynical joke? Was she going to do something to embarrass Deena?

When Mrs. Friedman handed Kathy her schedule, Deena thought she heard the teacher say, "I like your earring, Kathy."

After homeroom Deena went to speech and debate class. Even though it was only the first day, they had a mock debate and Deena won. The teacher, Mr. Doowarf, said he was impressed by her "confidence and persuasion" in front of everyone and asked her to join the debate squad. So far, except for having Kathy in homeroom, everything was going fine. No—better than fine. It was great!

Deena practically floated to her next class until she bumped into Kathy. They were both going into Mrs. Godfrey's English class.

"Quit following me around," Kathy muttered.

"Hey, you're following me!" Deena said softly. "Just don't talk to me and no one will know."

"Good idea," Kathy whispered as they split up and went their separate ways—Deena to the front of the class and Kathy to the back.

"Good morning, class," the teacher said. "I'm Mrs. Godfrey. Welcome back to Cranford High." She was a small woman in her sixties who seemed to have more energy than a cheerleader after six cups of coffee. Deena liked her immediately. The class laughed as Mrs. Godfrey began playing a game of tic-tac-toe on the blackboard with herself. "I'm sure you've heard many a rumor about me—I started most of them myself. However, I want you to know that I do have one rule upon which I insist. No cute or fuzzy little stuffed animals in class—I don't care how much Shakespeare they've read."

As Mrs. Godfrey talked about the course, Deena went row by row, writing down the names of people in class she had met already. Suddenly the teacher swooped down like a hawk and snatched Deena's open notebook away from her.

"What are you doing? Taking notes? During attendance?" Mrs. Godfrey asked. She looked at the page in shock. "It's a seating chart," she told the class. "What's your name, miss?"

"Deena Scott."

"A transfer student!" Mrs. Godfrey yelled as if she had just discovered a double agent. "Well, don't just sit there like a student! Tell us something about yourself."

Deena smiled, cleared her throat, and stood up facing the class. This was the moment she had been waiting for. She knew that teachers often asked new students to say something on their first day at a new school. So Deena had prepared what she would say the night before.

"Hello, I'm Deena Scott," she said. "I lived in Boston all my life until I moved to Cranford five days ago. And

I'm looking forward to this class because I'm going to be a writer someday."

"I'll be the judge of that," Mrs. Godfrey interrupted.

"People also say I'm a take-charge kind of person," Deena added with a winning smile.

"In that case maybe you'd better sit down before the class forgets about *me*," said Mrs. Godfrey.

Kathy cringed in the back of the room. How corny could Deena get? I'd rather die than *stand up* and make a cute little speech to the class. It's weird that no one else seems to think she's a dweeb.

Suddenly Mrs. Godfrey started walking toward Kathy.

"Where's the other new girl?" Mrs. Godfrey asked.

Kathy slid down lower in her seat, but it was no use. Mrs. Godfrey had spotted her.

"Aha!" Mrs. Godfrey said. "Well? What do you have to say for yourself, young lady?"

Kathy sat up a little bit and looked the strange teacher in the eyes.

"I'm Kathy Manelli," she said. "And I'm from San Francisco. At my old school new kids didn't have to give speeches. It was easier just to rope and brand them. You know—with a big NS for new student."

Deena wanted to melt into her backpack. Was she kidding? Making fun of the school on the first day? Deena couldn't even look at Kathy.

"And to look at them, you'd never guess they were cousins, would you, class?" asked Mrs. Godfrey.

Deena shot Kathy a quick glance and saw that her cousin was just as mortified as she was. How did Mrs. God-frey find out? And why didn't she keep her big mouth shut? All of a sudden Deena didn't love this crazy old teacher quite so much.

"You girls just moved into the old Cranberry Inn," Mrs. Godfrey went on. "Guess we'll have to call you two the Cranberry Cousins."

"Hey, you don't *have* to call us that," Kathy said a little too forcefully.

"Really," Deena agreed.

But the class's laughter gave the name an official stamp of approval. They were marked—inseparable forever, like death and taxes, smoke and fire, hit-and-run—the Cranberry Cousins.

By lunchtime Deena had heard the words *cranberry* and *cousin* used so often together that the phrase felt like a dentist's drill in her head. And it was the slow drill, not the high-speed one.

She moved her tray quietly through the cafeteria line, looking at the food halfheartedly.

Across from her and behind the steam tables stood a large woman with a kitchen serving spoon in each hand. She wore an apron with the name Lucille stitched on it.

"Turkey? It comes with cranberries," asked Lucille in a take-it-or-leave-it voice.

"No cranberries!" Deena said, maybe a little too sharply.

"Meat-loaf melt," Lucille said.

"I hate meat loaf," Deena said.

"Of course you do, hon," said Lucille. "I only made it

to torture you. How about ordering something so we can keep the line moving?"

"Give me meat-loaf melt," Deena said.

"Want some cranberries to sweeten it up?" Lucille asked.

"No!" Deena answered quickly.

Deena paid for her food, dumped her tray in the receptacle, and sat down at a table by herself with a carton of skim milk.

"Hi," said a friendly voice. It was Jessie Martin with two of her girl friends. "This is Tracey and Teddie," she said as the three girls sat down.

All three were exactly the same height. Jessie was the thinnest and the prettiest and her Cranford High School sweater matched the burgundy color of the clips in her reddish-blond hair. Tracey had jet black hair, a thin pale face, and dark circles under her eyes. Teddie seemed to put all of her energy into looking and acting older than she was.

"I guess everyone knows who you are by now," Tracey said.

"Hey, Deena," Jessie said, "your advice worked. Mr. Millander was almost human to me."

"You and your cousin, are, like, really opposites, aren't you?" Tracey said.

Deena nodded her head yes and sipped her milk.

"Good," Teddie said, almost with a sigh. "Although Kathy *was* pretty funny today. Did you hear what she did to Millander?"

Deena braced herself and shook her head no.

"She was chewing gum in Mr. Millander's class," Jessie said. "So he says to her: 'Miss Manelli. Would you please spit that out, unless you have enough for everyone.' So she reaches into her purse and starts pulling things out. You wouldn't believe what she has in there . . . tapes, three pairs of tights, a sandwich, enough make-up for a Broadway musical, a bicycle chain and lock . . . the stuff just kept coming out! Anyway, one by one she pulls out five enormous packs of gum. It was totally a riot. Millander about split a gut, but he let her pass it around, and I swear he almost even smiled."

"He didn't smile," Teddie said. "He was grinding his teeth."

"No, he smiled," Jessie insisted.

"Hey, listen, you guys, do you want to hear my news or not?" Teddie said. "Craig Leadford asked me to the Bexley Bonfire. Doesn't it just grieve you?"

Tracey and Jessie pounded the table.

"What's the Bexley Bonfire?" Deena asked.

"Well, everyone thinks it's this big pep rally thing that happens every year before the Cranford-Bexley football game," Tracey said between bites of meat loaf. "See, both towns make big bonfires and light them at exactly eight o'clock at night."

"And both schools make these big papier-mâché copies of the schools' mascots," Jessie said. "Like, our mascot is the fox, so we'll make a big papier-mâché fox. Then we hang it up somewhere in town, and they do the same thing with theirs."

"Right," Tracey went on. "And then just about everyone in Cranford drives over to Bexley to find the Bexley Lion and bring it back to burn in the bonfire. And they do the same to us. Whoever burns the other team's mascot first is supposed to have better luck in the football game."

"Blah, blah, blah. But you want to know what the Bexley Bonfire really is about?" Teddie said. Without waiting for an answer she added, "It's our first test of where we stand with the boys—especially the juniors and seniors."

"And Craig Leadford is a senior and a total hunk, no assembly required," Jessie explained to Deena. Then she turned back to Teddie. "He really asked you to go?"

Teddie just smiled and batted her long black eyelashes.

"A senior smiled and talked to me this morning," Deena said.

"Great! Who was he?" Jessie asked with a lot of interest.

"I don't know," Deena said. "I don't know anyone's name."

"I'll give you my yearbook from last year so you can learn who everyone is," Tracey offered.

"Really? Thanks a lot," Deena said. And she thought to herself, What a difference—being with girls who treat me like a human being!

"I'm on the committee to make the Cranford Fox for this year's bonfire," Teddie said. "You want to help out? In the gym after school."

"Thanks!" Deena said.

Warning bells all over the school began to ring, and the

girls immediately grabbed for their purses and books. Then they hurried off to class.

* * *

That night Deena lay on her bed writing in her journal. "He is the most charismatic speaker I have ever heard in my life," she said quietly, reading what she had just written.

There was no need for Kathy to stop sketching in her notebook to ask who her cousin was talking about. Deena had talked about nothing but her speech teacher, Mr. Doowarf, and the Bexley Bonfire ever since she got home.

"I met a lot of kids tonight while working on the bonfire committee," Deena said.

"I wonder if there will be as many tomorrow—when they find out you're coming back," Kathy muttered. She stood up to examine the dove trapped in the teardrop that was slowly appearing on her sketchpad.

"Ha, ha," Deena said without laughing. "What are you so mad about? What did I do?"

"Nothing."

"Is it because I get to stay out late working on the Cranford Fox for the bonfire?"

"That was the best part of the day," Kathy said without looking at Deena.

Deena adjusted her position so she could write sitting up, with her journal in her lap. "Well—since you're not going to be any help in this conversation, I'll have to rely on my powers of observation," Deena said. "I'd say you've been angry ever since last period in Ms. Zimmer's phys. ed. class. Is it because we weren't on the same volleyball team?"

"No."

"Are you mad because my team won?"

"No."

"Are you mad because my team won by a landslide?"

"No."

"Are you mad because I kept spiking the ball down your throat? It's just part of the game, you know. You should try harder."

"Forget it. O.K.?"

"You know what Ms. Zimmer said to me after the game?" Deena said, writing as she spoke.

"No—all I know is what she said to me. 'Kathy, you should try to be more like your cousin. Now *there's* a really superb athlete!'" Kathy said, imitating the gym teacher's voice. Then she stormed out of the bedroom and slammed the door.

Chapter 4

The next week flew by. Each day after school Deena worked on the Cranberry Fox with her new friends. Little by little the mascot, which was made out of papier-mâché and brown, torn tissue paper, took shape.

At the same time the Cranberry Inn was beginning to get into shape, too. Not a great shape, but a shape.

But that was no thanks at all to Kathy, Deena thought as she set the dinner table by herself for the third night in a row. Somehow Kathy was just never around when the windows needed to be caulked, the floors waxed, the oven scrubbed, or the table set. She cut classes at school. Why shouldn't she cut "home," too?

Deena grumbled quietly. Knife and spoon on the right.

Napkin on the left. Fork on napkin—hm, that fork's not completely clean.

Deena put that one at Kathy's place.

Just then Johnny came into the kitchen and set his baseball bat and mitt on the long wooden table next to his napkin and fork.

"Johnny, baseball stuff doesn't really belong at the table," Deena said.

"Strike two. Last night you said I couldn't read at the table," Johnny said. "What am I supposed to do for fun?"

"Hey—you can eat and make interesting conversation," Deena said. "That's what families do."

"Not in San Francisco, we didn't," Johnny said. Then he added real quickly, "But don't say it. I know. This *isn't* San Francisco."

"You learn quickly," Deena said with a smile.

"I guess I have *you* fooled, anyway," Johnny said, taking his baseball gear away from the table.

"Hey! What does that mean?" Deena called.

But he was out the door too fast.

It was more fun arguing with him than with his sister. At least he had a normal sense of humor.

One Manelli walked out and another walked in.

"Hi, guys," Kathy said.

"Kath, where've you been?" her mother called from the sink, where she was finishing the salad.

She's going to say: Just walking, Mom, Deena said to herself. And Aunt Nancy is going to drop it right there.

"Just walking, Mom," Kathy said.

"Uh-huh," her mother answered.

41

"Looks like I'm too late to set the table, huh?"

"Your timing is perfect," Deena said.

"Why are we eating in the kitchen?" Kathy asked.

"Well, if you took fewer walks, you'd know the latest episode in the Cranberry Inn story," Deena said.

"We've got our first customers, Kath," Nancy explained. She brought the large salad to the table. "Sit down, everybody. Oh, Deena, tell your mom dinner's ready, if she can tear herself away from her computer."

"Watch this, " Deena said. She opened the kitchen door and imitated Kathy's voice perfectly. "Aunt Lydia! Chow!"

"Coming, Kathy," Lydia called back.

"Very funny," Kathy said. "Why don't you go taste the soup—just stick your head in the pot."

"Mellow out, Kath," Nancy said. "It was a pretty good imitation of you. But actually, we've got to cool it around here with the yelling, now that we have paying guests."

"Who are they?" Kathy asked. "I thought we weren't open for business for another month."

Johnny came in and sat down, followed by Lydia.

"Smells and looks great, Nancy," Lydia said.

"Can I get an answer around here?" Kathy insisted.

"Yes," her mother said calmly. "This afternoon an elderly couple, Mr. and Mrs. Schuster, drove up. They said they came to this inn every year in September for twenty-five years, until the inn closed. Well, they heard that it was opening up again and they said they didn't mind a little dust. They wanted to be here for their anniversary. They were so cute."

"In other words your mother couldn't say no to them," Lydia teased. "So ready or not, from now on we're acting as if we run the place."

Deena admired how her mother could bring the curtain down on a conversation.

"How was school today, Kath?" Nancy asked.

"Ask Deena. Maybe she'll write an essay about it."

Here we go, Deena thought. If you live on a fault line, you've got to expect earthquakes. And why was everyone just waiting for *Deena* to explain Kathy's remark?

"I think Kathy is talking about what happened in English class today," Deena said. "I read my critical essay on T. S. Eliot's poem 'The Waste Land' to the class."

"Two kids died of old age while she was reading it," Kathy said.

"The main thing is that Mrs. Godfrey said it displayed a keen insight into the writing process," Deena said.

"It should definitely go into a time capsule," Kathy grumbled. "That way no one else will have to listen to it for another hundred years!"

The conversation went on like that throughout dinner—a little on the tense side but not an all-out hostility match.

Deena finally left the table before dessert. She couldn't take it anymore. She went upstairs to her room, sat at her desk, and began writing in her journal. It was the one way she could say whatever she wanted and no one would take sides.

A few mintues later Deena heard footsteps and the rat-

43

tle of forks on plates. She looked up and saw Kathy with two plates of cake.

"You want some?" she asked.

"Sure," Deena said, amazed as always by Kathy's changing moods.

We're sitting on opposite sides of the room, Deena thought. You'd think we were afraid to breathe the same air.

"Everyone downstairs thinks I shouldn't have cut down your essay during dinner," Kathy said.

"It's all right," Deena said. "I know how you feel." But when she saw Kathy's clouding face, she quickly took that back. "Sorry—I *don't* know how you feel. No one in the *whole world* knows how you feel, O.K.? But guess what? *You* don't know how I feel, either."

"Hey—cool out. I just brought you cake, didn't I? Give me a break here," Kathy said. She smiled her sweetest smile at Deena and licked icing off her fork.

Deena wrote a few more paragraphs and then sneaked a look at Kathy. At times like this Deena almost felt like they could be friends. Was it worth taking a chance and asking Kathy for a favor?

Deena decided to risk it.

"You know there's a big pep rally tomorrow after sixth period," Deena said.

"Yeah," Kathy said.

"You going?"

"I don't know. Are you?"

"I don't know," Deena said. "I don't really want to go alone."

"What happened to the three stooges—Jessie, Tracey, and Teddie?"

Deena's eyes narrowed. Maybe this wasn't the time to take a chance. "They're cheerleaders," she said. "They'll be busy tomorrow. I was going to ask if you wanted to meet me and we'd sit together, but forget it. I just won't go."

"Hey, ease up. I'll go with you, Deena. O.K.?"

"Really?"

"Sure," Kathy said, flashing that smile again.

"Great—thanks!" Deena said. "I mean, I know it's immature, but I just didn't want to walk in all alone, cheer alone, you know? I think it's really impossible to participate in a group ritual like cheering when the people standing on both sides of you are complete strangers."

"Spare me the sociological commentary," Kathy said. "I already said I'll go. Just don't expect me to make that Cranford Fox sound."

"Agreed," Deena said. "Now, let's see. I think we should meet by the water fountain outside the gym after sixth period. What are you going to wear?"

"I'll find something," Kathy said.

Deena looked at Kathy's side of the room. Her floor and bed were piled high with clothes—all of them wrinkled.

How is she going to find something in that mess? Deena wondered.

"We need more drawer space," Deena said out loud. "So we can clean this place up."

"Hey—if you're so into drawer space, why don't you work on stripping that old chest of drawers?" Kathy said.

By myself? Deena thought. No way. I'm already doing more than my share of the chores around here. Let's see you put in a little effort, Manelli.

"I will if you will," Deena said pointedly.

"I already started on it," Kathy said. "I stripped all the drawer fronts last week." And on that perfect exit line, Kathy got up and left the room.

Kathy was certainly full of surprises, Deena thought.

* * *

The next day dragged by for Kathy like a car out of gas. First period—homeroom. Sit in the back and listen to some nerd reading the announcements on the P.A. Meanwhile, everyone else passed notes back and forth or crammed to finish the homework they should have done the night before. Of course, Deena didn't engage in such childish activities. She just sat in the front row quietly writing in that journal of hers.

Second period dragged, too. Biology. It was supposed to be a lab class, which Kathy would have liked. But so far all they'd done was make a drawing of the circulatory system. Boring, boring, boring with a capital B.

Third period was English with Deena and old lady Godfrey.

Fourth was French. Mademoiselle Kathy—*Dormez-vous*? Am I sleeping? *Oui, Madame*. I sure am. And I'd sleep a whole lot better if you didn't keep asking me questions!

Then came lunch. Still no friends—no one to talk to. There were a lot of cool-looking kids in the school, but they didn't seem to eat in the cafeteria. Maybe they went out for lunch—but Kathy didn't know where.

By the end of sixth period, which was Health Education, Kathy was seriously thinking about bringing a pillow to school.

RINNGG! That was the bell. An announcement came over the P.A. reminding everyone that the pep rally was next. "Immediately following the pep rally," the announcement said, "all students are expected to report to their seventh-period classes."

Kathy took her time walking down a couple of flights of stairs on her way to the gym to meet Deena. It was weird for the halls to be so empty. Hey—where is everyone? After a few minutes Kathy realized that she was lost. Cranford High was a fairly big school and certain sections were still a mystery to her.

She stopped on some stairs and listened. Voices were mumbling and laughing nearby. She walked down a few steps and peered over the railing. Three kids were sitting in the stairwell one flight down.

One of them, Ellecia Spink, was a girl Kathy sort of knew. She was a short, pretty sophomore with long black hair except for the shock of bright blue in front that kept falling over her right eye. Kathy had seen her fake the hiccups in class several times, just to make her teachers nuts.

The other girl Kathy didn't know, but she'd seen her

around. She had stringy blond hair moussed out like a fright wig.

And the guy—the guy was really cute. His hair was spiky on top and short on the sides. Kathy liked his leather jacket and his earring, too.

"Hey!" Kathy said, walking downstairs.

"What's happening?" Ellecia said.

"Where'd they move the gym?" Kathy asked with a laugh.

"You mean you're going to the pep rally?" the guy asked.

"I'm looking for the gym," Kathy said. "I can say what I mean."

The guy put his hands up in the air, as if giving up to the police.

"Come on, Roy," Ellecia said. "Kathy's O.K."

"Yeah, it's her cousin who's the . . . " The blond-haired girl looked for a way to express herself. Finally she just pretended to put her finger down her throat.

"Zee, you're awful," Ellecia said.

But Kathy laughed. "I'm supposed to be meeting . . . uh, someone outside the gym," she said.

"What do you like the best about the pep rally? The cheers or the pompom girls?" Zee asked.

"The marching band," Kathy said sarcastically. "I've got all their tapes." She took some gum out of her bag. "Want some?" she said, offering it to Roy.

"Yeah, and we know—you've got enough for everyone!" Zee said, laughing. She grabbed a stick of gum for herself.

Kathy smiled. She was glad that everyone had heard about the scene in Mr. Millander's classroom.

"So you're from San Francisco, huh," Ellecia said to Kathy. "What's it like there?"

"It's pretty freaky. A lot of garage bands. I sang with one," Kathy said. "We were good, too, before I left."

"Oh, yeah?" Roy said. He struck a pose holding an air guitar and sang a few lyrics of a popular song. When he stopped, Kathy picked it up where he left off. For once she didn't have to keep it down because Deena was studying, or talking on the phone, or breathing. And it felt great to be singing again. The hallway had fabulous acoustics, and Ellecia, Roy, and Zee looked really impressed when she was done.

"Wow," Ellecia said. "Awesome."

Zee made a place on the steps for Kathy to sit down. And for the first time since she had arrived in Cranford, Kathy relaxed. She and Ellecia talked about music and how they needed more music at Cranford, and wouldn't Mr. Millander look genuinely awesome in a spiky toupee. And Zee made nasty comments about half the kids in the school whenever someone's name came up.

Roy didn't do too much talking, though. In fact, it took ten minutes for Kathy to find out that he was a junior— and another ten to find out he had a motorcycle. He looked as if he felt weird about being the only guy standing around talking to three girls. Like he was outnumbered or something. But Kathy thought he also looked like he wanted to stay—because of her.

For a minute Kathy's mind flashed on Deena and the

pep rally. But then she figured it was too late. Deena had probably already gone in. Besides—what was more important: sitting in the gym with your cousin or making new friends?

Anyway, this was too much fun. Ellecia was doing her hiccups and a noise that sounded just like a cat throwing up. She wore this fabulous silver skull ring, too. And sometimes she talked to it and called it Harry.

After a while Zee mentioned the Bexley Bonfire. Kathy jokingly clamped her hand over Zee's mouth. "Give me a break. I hear about it all the time at home—from my cousin," she said.

"Football is nothing," Roy said. "But the bonfire is great. Like, no money changes hands. It's nice. Everyone just parties all night. You should go."

"Definitely," Ellecia said.

Hey, are they asking me to go with them? Kathy wondered. That would be so great. But she couldn't exactly tell if that's what Roy meant.

"I'll think about it," Kathy said.

Roy just shrugged.

"Well, I gotta go," he said. "Catch you later, Manelli."

Sounds good to me, Kathy thought.

Now . . . later . . . anytime.

Chapter 5

Late Friday afternoon, after the pep rally, Deena sat in her room ignoring the warm sunshine that rolled through the windows like a surfer's wave, and not seeing the dazzling autumn leaves. She was oblivious to everything outside her own small world. She sat on her bed listening to sad Simon and Garfunkel songs.

"I used to have great friends," she said to the photograph on the album cover. "We respected each other. And when someone said they would do something, they did it."

Deena got out her scrapbook, volume five, the one all her friends had signed before she left Boston.

To my best friend Deena,

Without your friendship, I am incomplete. I can inhale but not exhale. I'll send you all of my rough drafts. No one understands my poetry the way you do. Be wonderful.

Ginnie

Hey, Deena—

Why don't you get lost—so I can find you. Keep warm in Cranford (wherever that is). We'll miss you.

Sam

Deena,

What would I have done without you? You've been right about everything. Thanks for all your good advice. I'm sure I'll get used to the crewcut, too. Be good.

Gregg

A voice ripped through her memories like fingernails screeching across a blackboard. "Mom said you wanted something. What's going on?" Kathy asked. She came in chewing an apple and flopped down on her bed.

Deena snapped off the record player. "How could you do that to me?" she said.

"How could I do what? Ask you what's going on?" Kathy looked as if she didn't have a clue why Deena was mad.

Deena edged closer to the invisible line down the middle of the room, dividing her half from Kathy's. "No! How could you not show up at the pep rally?"

"I got lost. I couldn't find the gym. I didn't think you'd freak out."

"Freak out!!" Deena shouted. "Do you know what it's like to have the entire school walk past you and go into the gym while you're standing there like a complete idiot?"

"What's it like?" Kathy asked.

"While everyone is in there, cheering and clapping and admiring the Cranford Fox, which *I* helped to make with my own hands, I'm standing outside—waiting for my cousin! I might as well have been waiting for the tooth fairy!"

"I got lost. And then I ran into some kids. I thought you'd go in without me," Kathy said.

"I didn't go in!" Deena shouted and stomped her foot. "I was too mortified! Do you know what I did?! I left school. I *cut* my classes! And I've never done that in my life."

"Oh, wow. There goes your shot at Supreme Court justice." Kathy pushed some clothes off her bed so she'd have more room.

"It's not a joke!" Deena yelled, picking up the pile of Kathy's clothes and throwing them back at Kathy. "The only joke around here is how you live your life."

"Deena!"

It was Deena's mom, Lydia, standing in the doorway. Her face was serious and pale. "What's the matter with

53

you two? We have *guests*, remember? Mr. and Mrs. Schuster just complained about all the noise and yelling up here."

"Oh, let them turn down their hearing aids," Kathy said. "We have rights, too. This is our home."

"No," Lydia said, her arms folded over her chest. "This is our *business*. And *our* customers come first. Do you understand that I don't expect any more outbursts like this?"

Deena answered her mother sullenly. "Yes." Sure. There wouldn't be any more outbursts. But there wouldn't be any more trusting, either. As far as Deena was concerned, she was through with Kathy. She had given her her last chance.

* * *

The next day was Saturday. It was the day Johnny named the Invasion of the Cats. The five kittens who lived with their mother in the attic began climbing down the stairs to explore the world. They were rolling and running everywhere. You couldn't walk anywhere without almost stepping on one of them. Kathy and Johnny sat down to play with them in the first-floor sitting room in front of the fireplace.

"I'm going to give them baseball names during baseball season and football names later," Johnny said.

"You can't do that," Kathy said, trying to pet the

tummy of a squirming, wrestling kitten. "What if I called you by different names?"

"You call me lots of names all the time," Johnny said.

Kathy pulled her brother's baseball cap down over his face.

"You want to hear about the catcher's mitt I picked out?" he asked.

"You told me fifteen minutes ago," Kathy said, picking up the kitten that was climbing her arm. "Relax. We'll buy it later."

Outside there was the roar of a motorcycle engine revving up once before it was turned off. Kathy wanted to jump up and look out the window. There was only one person she knew in Cranford who drove a motorcycle—Roy Harris, the guy Kathy had met the day before in the stairwell. But she couldn't move. She was too nervous.

Johnny jumped up and ran to the front door as soon as the bell rang. There was Roy, wearing a silver-studded black leather jacket, black jeans, a white shirt and a long narrow black tie.

"Where'd you come from? MTV?" Johnny asked.

Roy took off his sunglasses. Then he peered into the room and saw Kathy with three kittens in her lap, sitting near the fireplace.

"Hey," he called to her. "How's it going?"

O.K., calm down, Kathy told herself. He's just a hunk—I mean a guy. But what's he doing here? Who cares! Just say something before he goes away.

"Hi. Want a kitten?" Kathy said to Roy.

"No, thanks, I already ate," Roy said. And then in a quick move, he pulled Johnny's legs out from under him.

Johnny laughed when he found himself suddenly sitting on his bottom.

"So, you ever been married or anything like that?" Roy said, walking over to Kathy.

Kathy tried not to giggle, because it didn't look cool. But she couldn't help it. That's what was special about Roy. You never knew what he was going to say or do next.

"A kid proposed to me once in sixth grade," Kathy answered. "He said we could live in his tree house. Said he was making O.K. money on his paper route," she added with a straight face.

"No kidding," Roy said.

"Yeah." Kathy gave him her best smile and tossed her hair back so her earring would show more. Roy laughed.

"You're a great addition to Cranford, Manelli. I'll tell you that," he said.

Kathy beamed.

"So," she said. "Your bike out front?" Of course, it's his bike, you bozo. You think he stole it?

"Most of it," Roy said.

"Can I have a ride?" Johnny asked.

"Johnny, beat it," Kathy said.

"I don't want to," Johnny said, looking up at Roy as if he were a tree.

"Two words, Johnny, and you know what they mean," Kathy said. "Baseball mitt."

"I'm out of here," Johnny said, running for the door, which closed with a bang.

Roy started playing with a fat kitten, trying to teach it to do the moonwalk. Then he turned back to Kathy and said, "Want to go . . . "

To the Bexley Bonfire with you? Say the words, please say them.

" . . . for a ride?"

"Yeah. Sure. Great."

Just as Kathy stood up, she saw Deena coming downstairs.

"Let's go," Kathy said to Roy.

"Where are you going?" Deena said, putting her hands on her hips.

"Riding," Kathy said.

"Where?"

"On the back of Roy's bike, *Mom*," Kathy said. "Roy, this is my mother."

Roy nodded at Deena. "Hi, Mom," he said.

"Don't you have to check with your mother, Kathy?" Deena asked.

"She's not here."

"Well, mine is," Deena said.

"Then *you* check with her when you're going out," Kathy said.

"Now what?" asked Lydia, walking through with fresh sheets for the guest room.

"Aunt Lydia, I'm going for a ride with Roy."

"Where are you going?" Deena asked.

Kathy threw her hands up. "To the moon."

"I'd better buy some more gas," Roy said.

"Kathy, is that his motorcycle out front?" Lydia said.

"Yes," Kathy said, sensing doom.

"Well, I don't know . . . " Lydia said. "Do you have an extra helmet for Kathy, Roy?"

"No, but she can wear mine," Roy said.

"But then you won't have one. No, I don't think it's safe. I'm sorry Kathy. I don't want you to go," Lydia said.

"What?" Kathy shouted. "My mom would let me."

"If your mom says it's O.K., that's fine for next time," Lydia said. "But she's not here. *I* am. And I can't take the responsibility. As far as I'm concerned, motorcycles aren't safe."

"Sure they are," Roy said. "Unless you go down."

Why did he have to be so honest right now?

"That's not a risk I'm willing to take," Lydia said.

"I'm not taking a risk. It's a ride!!"

"Not on the motorcycle, Kathy. I'm sorry."

Kathy glared at Deena as if this were all her fault. No ride. No Bexley Bonfire. No Roy. What were Deena and Aunt Lydia trying to do to her? "You're not sorry at all," she said to her aunt in a desperate whisper. "Do you want him to think I'm just a stupid little kid?"

It was obvious from Lydia's face that she wasn't used to this kind of family discussion.

"I'm sure if he's the boy you think he is, he'll know that *I'm* the villain here—not you, Kathy," her aunt said softly.

"I can't go right now, Roy," Kathy said, turning back

to face him. She was having a hard time controlling her voice. "Try again when these people know it's the twentieth century."

"Yeah, sure. Well, catch you later, Manelli," he said, turning to leave.

Kathy watched from the door as Roy rode out of the driveway in a blast of noise.

As soon as he was gone, she turned around. "You're not going to tell me what to do!" she shouted at Lydia.

"I *will* tell you what to do," Lydia said in a voice that was too calm and too soft. "And the first thing I'm telling you is to lower your voice, Kathy."

Kathy stomped up to the third floor as loud as she could and slammed the door to her room. Almost instantly a Nuclear Waste tape began to shake the foundation of the old inn.

Deena looked at Johnny, who had returned and was sitting very still on the floor trying to hold all five kittens in his lap. He looked as if he wanted to hide. Deena sat down beside him, but he pulled away.

Lydia looked at her daughter and nephew. "Sometimes," she said, "it takes a team a little while to play together well. They've got to learn all the signals and all the plays, you know."

"Kathy wants to be a free agent," Johnny said.

His aunt laughed. "I don't know what that is in baseball, but I'm sure you're right."

"She was going to take me to buy a new catcher's mitt today," Johnny said.

"Don't worry. I'll take you," Deena said.

"She'll be mad if you do," Johnny said.

"She's always mad," Deena said. "That doesn't mean you shouldn't get your mitt, does it?"

Chapter 6

It was almost dinnertime when Deena and Johnny came back to the Cranberry Inn from shopping at the mall. Things had changed while they were away. The front yard had been cleaned up. All the twigs, branches, and leaves from the trees in the yard had been carried away. And Deena's attitude had improved, too. She'd been away from her cousin long enough that she was actually looking forward to being home again.

Welcoming lights were turned on in the downstairs rooms.

Deena stopped at the foot of the winding driveway to

look at her new home. "It's a beautiful old house, isn't it?" she said to Johnny.

"Yeah," Johnny said, rushing into the house to show his new glove to his mother, his aunt, Kathy, and to the guests, Mr. and Mrs. Schuster. When no one else was left, he showed it to the kittens sleeping in the attic.

A few minutes later Deena came inside, too. But as soon as she stepped into the kitchen, she wanted to leave again. Something was cooking—and it wasn't just the dinner. Lydia and Nancy were doing what Deena called a kitchen ballet, crossing in front of each other, moving quickly from sink to stove, not bumping into each other—and not saying a word to each other.

"Oh, hi, Deena," Nancy said. "Thanks for taking Johnny to the mall."

"Water's boiling," Lydia said.

"I know the water's boiling," Nancy said, moving to the stove with a bowl of fresh pasta. "How about the sauce?"

"I'm working on it," Lydia said.

"Why are you cutting up the tomatoes so small?" Nancy said, looking over her sister's shoulder.

"Don't *you*?" Lydia said. "Mom always did."

"Well, no, I don't," Nancy said. "But it'll be super."

"Thanks," Lydia said with a chill.

Deena wished there were something she could say to break the tension and make the situation better. But she didn't know what the tension was about. So she went upstairs to wash.

Kathy was lying on her bed like a corpse.

"You know, you could help out once in a while around here," Deena said. "Our mothers are down there making dinner all by themselves."

"I cleaned up the whole front yard today," Kathy said curtly. "And I ache all over."

"Something weird is going on downstairs," Deena said.

"Your mom making liver croquettes again?"

"No, but I think you ought to lay off the wisecracks tonight!"

Kathy looked ready to explode. "First you tell me what to wear and what to do. Then your mom tells me where I can and can't go. Now you want to tell me what to say? Go eat a golf ball," Kathy said as she jumped off her bed.

She headed down the back stairway with Deena following. But when they got to the bottom, they froze. Johnny was standing by the closed kitchen door, listening to their mothers arguing in the kitchen. Both girls listened, too.

"The point is you weren't here, Nancy!" Lydia said sharply. "So I had to make a decision."

"I know that," Nancy said. "I just wish you had made a different decision. Really, you know I wouldn't have sweated it if she'd gone for a motorcycle ride. I mean, Cranford isn't exactly the fast track, you know. But I had to back you up—otherwise it looks like no one's in charge around here. So I told her she's not allowed to ride around on that boy's motorcycle. She was devastated and miserable, and I don't even know why I'm making the rule."

63

"I can think of several good reasons," Lydia said. "Besides, you're too lenient with her. You just want her to have the life you didn't have."

"Go to your room, Johnny," Kathy whispered to her brother.

"But I'm hungry," he complained.

"I have some Halloween candy in my room with my socks," Kathy said.

"It's a month early," Johnny said.

"Then go upstairs and wait a month!" Kathy hissed, pointing her brother in the right direction.

"Shhh!" Deena whispered.

"Don't tell me how to raise my children," they heard Nancy say.

"You told *me* how to make spaghetti sauce," Lydia answered.

Nancy sighed. "Look, we said this was going to be tough. We're different. We always have been."

Lydia waited a moment before answering.

"The Schusters left today," she said. "They said they were *never* coming back to this lunatic asylum," said Lydia.

There was a long silence. Kathy and Deena could easily imagine that Nancy was stunned by this news.

"It was your idea to run the inn together," Nancy said.

"I know. I thought things would be different," Lydia said. Another long silence.

"Well . . . maybe you'd be happier if we went back to San Francisco," Nancy said.

"I don't know," Lydia said without any emotion. "All

I know is that we can't run an inn if the customers leave and never come back. We've got to make this place pay."

Deena and Kathy backed away from the kitchen door and sat down on the back steps.

Deena's face looked chalky. "What are you smiling about?" she said when she saw Kathy's expression. "That was awful. I've *never* heard my mother talk like that."

"Oh, sure," Kathy said. "Your mom just about asked my mom to leave—and you're worried about *your* mom's feelings?"

"My mom didn't mean it," Deena said. "She's just a little tense, that's all. Why are you *smiling*?"

"Because my mom just said the magic words," Kathy said, grinning. "*Back to San Francisco.*"

* * *

Deena and Kathy sat through dinner in silence, and everyone pretended. The cousins pretended they hadn't overheard their mothers' fight. Nancy and Lydia pretended they hadn't said hurtful things to each other. And Johnny pretended he hadn't eaten five candy bars right before dinner.

But as soon as dinner was over and Kathy could get away without arousing suspicion, she threw on her jacket and headed out of the inn.

Well, thanks a lot for the pep talk, Aunt Lydia, Kathy thought as she crunched through fallen leaves. But too bad you forgot to ask the primo question: Do we all really seriously want this to work out? Maybe you don't know

65

it, but there is one person who'd be a lot happier if we went back to San Francisco, and things went back to the way they used to be. Even if it meant eating macaroni and cheese every night again.

Kathy counted the change in her pocket as she walked into town to make a phone call.

Sure the Cranberry Inn had telephones. Lots of them. But the Cranberry Inn also had ears everywhere you looked. Deena ears. Johnny ears. Mommy ears. Auntie ears. Little kitten ears. This was one telephone call Kathy wanted to make without being overheard.

She found a public telephone outside the post office just across from the town square. When she stepped into the fluorescent booth, her long spangled sweater sparkled in the light. Kathy dialed a number and then started dropping quarters in the phone for what seemed like hours. It took a lot of quarters to call San Francisco.

The phone rang twice.

"Hello?" said a teenager's voice on the other end.

Kathy knew that voice instantly. Jenn Kahn. And suddenly it felt as if they were only three blocks apart, the way they had been most of their lives. Kathy even laughed to hear Jenn's loud breathing in the phone. She always held the mouthpiece too close to her mouth.

"Jenn? I can't believe it!" Kathy said. "Hi. This is your long-lost best friend."

"Kathy!" Jenn shouted. "How's it going? What's happening? How's Cranapple or whatever it's called?"

"Cranford," Kathy said. "It's a nice place to visit, but

66

you wouldn't want to live here. Johnny loves it, and I met an incredible guy who wanted me to ride on his motorcycle. And the old house is wild but it's a mess. How's the band?"

"It's, you know, it's O.K."

"Can't get along without me, huh?"

"Well, you know, yeah, of course. How are you? And how's your cousin?" Jenn asked.

Kathy knew Jenn was trying to change the subject, but she didn't know why.

"My cousin and I are totally World War Three," Kathy said. "And my mom and Aunt Lydia are World War Three and a half. So, great news: I might be moving back to California—soon! My mom's going to give up on this place. And when I get back, we can really get the band going this time."

"Oh, that's really great." Jenn mumbled it more than she said it.

The phone almost slipped out of Kathy's hand. Come on, Jenn. This is Kathy with the x-ray eyes. I can see how you're standing right now. I know what you're doing. You're twisting your hair if you're telling the truth. But I'll bet you're twisting the telephone cord because something's wrong.

"What's going on?" Kathy asked.

"Hey, when you get back, Kath, are you going to get back with the band, like, right away?"

"No, that was my plan for after I die," Kathy said. "The record will go platinum and I'll go mold."

Jenn laughed and then sort of stammered. "See, like, we thought—we said we were going to make it without a singer, you know?"

"Yeah, that's what everyone said." Kathy waited. Here comes the truth, she prepared herself.

"But, it just wasn't good, Kath," Jenn said. She took a deep breath, "Look, I'm sorry, Kath. We got a new singer. She's dynamite. Not like you, you know. But it's working really good."

"But that's *my* band," Kathy said. "You guys said—"

"Yeah, but, you didn't want us to just fall apart or something, did you? And I mean, it wouldn't be fair to just dump her after we've worked so hard. You'll hear us when you come back. It's different, but it's good."

"Deposit seventy-five cents for the next three minutes," interrupted a tape-recorded voice.

I wouldn't give you a dime for three more minutes of this, Kathy thought.

"I'm out of money, Jenn," Kathy said. "I'll call you sometime."

"Yeah. Hey, Kath, I'm sorry, you know? I guess, things have to keep going, huh," Jenn said.

"Yeah," Kathy said after she hung up. "Till they hit bottom." She walked back to the inn.

Deena was in her nightgown and robe, sitting at her desk, doing a mountain of homework. And she looked almost as if she were enjoying it. Kathy wondered what would happen if her cousin's Duracells ever ran down.

"You got a call," Deena said.

"Roy?"

68

"Ellecia," Deena said. "You also got some mail." Deena handed Kathy a folded note.

Kathy opened the note, written in Johnny's nine-year-old squiggly handwriting.

Dear Kathy,
I hate you. You ruined everything.
Love,
Johnny

Poor Johnny, Kathy thought. He loves this old house so much. For him it's just kittens and rooms to hide in and dark places to pretend you're lost in. He doesn't have to live up here—with her.

"It was slipped under the door," Deena said. "I guess he thinks you guys are going back to San Francisco. Anyway, I hope they have a remedial handwriting program at Johnny's school."

Typical, Kathy thought. He pours his heart out, and all she can do is comment on his penmanship.

"Going for another walk now?" Deena said somewhat hopefully.

"It doesn't always help," Kathy said. In fact, it didn't help at all. Forget San Francisco, Kathy decided. There was nothing back there for her anymore. She *had* to make it work here—even with Deena.

"Listen," Kathy said cautiously to Deena. "I want to ask you something. How do you think this is going? I mean us—sharing this room. Be honest."

"Honestly? Well, so far," Deena said, moving onto her

69

bed, "I'd put it somewhere between my first taste of eggplant and the time I fell backward off the sliding board ladder when I was seven."

Kathy smiled. "I did that, too," she said. "But I mean, do you ever think about going back home?"

"Mom says Boston is where we used to live," Deena said.

"For once forget what your mother says," Kathy said seriously. "I'm asking *you*. Do you ever wish you could go back to Boston?"

"Sometimes," Deena said. "Do you?"

"Do I wish you'd go back to Boston? Yeah, all the time."

It just came popping out, like most of the things Kathy said. And the minute she said it, she wanted to take it back. After all—she was trying to get along better with Deena!

But before Kathy could apologize or explain, Deena fell over on her back. It took a moment for Kathy to realize that instead of crying or throwing a fit, Deena was laughing. She was laughing so hard she couldn't stop. She was rolling on her bed, clutching her pillow.

"What's so funny?" Kathy asked.

"I don't know," Deena answered, still laughing like a fool. "Jessie says you look like you have your hair cut with grass clippers."

Kathy started to giggle, but mostly because Deena was laughing so hard. "Jessie could fall in a hole and not be missed for years," she said and laughed.

She threw a pillow and hit Deena smack in the face.

Deena howled.

Fwap! While Kathy was laughing, Deena threw her pillow back at her.

Gradually the laughing had to stop because their sides hurt too much. But it was fun while it lasted. Then they were quiet again, except for a few painful sighs as they caught their breath.

"Wouldn't our moms die if they heard us?" Deena said.

"We don't have to tell them," Kathy said. "Why get their hopes up?"

"Wouldn't they die if they knew we heard *them* fighting before dinner?" Deena said. Then she suddenly remembered the subject of the conversation. "Hey—do you want to move back to San Francisco?"

"No, San Francisco is where I used to have a band, that's all," Kathy said. "Listen, I thought maybe we could try to stop arguing. At least in front of everybody."

Deena laughed. "O.K., and if we really *have* to fight about something, we could excuse ourselves very politely, leave the room, and go somewhere else to tear each other's eyes out."

Deena was being silly, but Kathy thought maybe everything could be all right. She started giggling again.

"What's so funny?" Deena said with a laugh she tried to keep in so it came out a snort.

"I don't know. You are. You're almost losing it again!" Kathy moaned, holding her sides.

The telephone rang and Deena answered it.

"It's for you," she said, handing the phone to Kathy. "It's Ellecia. She wants to borrow your grass clippers!"

Fwap!!

"You missed me!" Deena screamed.

Kathy smiled at her cousin as she took the phone. For a second she put her hand over the mouthpiece so Ellecia wouldn't hear.

"Truce?" she whispered to Deena.

"Truce."

Chapter 7

"**I** am a gentle swan," Deena said to herself. "Hmmm, I am a fuchsia swan," she said, looking down at her pink leotard and sky-blue tights. She was dancing, and the music from the *Swan Lake* ballet filled the third-floor bedroom. It was the Sunday morning after the truce. So far, so good. At least no one was screaming yet.

Deena danced lightly around the room, turning on her toes and jumping over Kathy's piles of clothes when she came to them.

"Ouch!" Kathy suddenly cried from the bathroom.

"What happened?" Deena called. She clicked off her cassette player.

Kathy stuck her head out of the small bathroom adjoining their room. "I'm trying to put on my make-up, and I keep banging my head on the ceiling," she said.

"I know! I do that all the time," Deena said, glad to find something she and Kathy had in common. "It's because the roof slants."

"I know *why* it happens," Kathy said.

Kathy put her hands on her hips in a certain way which always warned Deena that a zinger was coming and to expect its arrival shortly.

"Remember what we said last night," Deena cautioned. "No fighting."

Kathy lowered her hands and went back into the bathroom. "I know *why* it happens. I want to know how to avoid it."

"Easy. Walk into the bathroom on your knees," Deena suggested.

"Huh? Then I couldn't see the mirror."

"You said you didn't want to bump your head," Deena laughed. "You didn't say anything about seeing the mirror, too."

"Very funny," Kathy said. "This stupid light bulb isn't bright enough, either. I can't see anything. Hey—I'm thinking about getting another earring."

"That's good. Then your ears would match," Deena said.

"No—another one in the same ear, Deena," Kathy sighed.

Deena went on dancing, even without the music. But

while she did, she scooped up a pile of Kathy's clothes and stuffed them into a laundry bag.

"It's a beautiful day," Deena said. "And I *love* our truce."

"Turning that music off helped about five hundred percent," called the voice in the bathroom.

"But *Swan Lake* is so romantic," Deena said, stuffing the next pile of clothes into the laundry bag. "I'll bet Nuclear Waste never sang anything about magical swans."

"Wrong," Kathy said. She started to sing a heavy blues song:

> "Drivin' down the roads,
> running over roads,
> a bird hit my windshield
> and broke its stupid neck!"

"You're right," Deena said. "How could I say they weren't romantic?"

"Wow!" Kathy said. "This bathroom has great acoustics! If I start a new band, we'll definitely have to rehearse in here."

"You'll have to get a very short band," Deena said.

Kathy came out of the bathroom. She was not what Deena would call dressed for fall. There was nothing faded or muted about Kathy's long black sweatshirt and red ski tights. Wasn't it just like Kathy to try to fight nature?

"What are you doing to my stuff?" Kathy asked, staring at Deena.

"I'm being helpful! Putting your dirty clothes in the laundry," Deena said. "We've got to do a wash."

"Those *aren't* my dirty clothes," Kathy said. She turned and pointed at a different pile. "Those are."

"Oh, sorry," Deena said. "Maybe you should put up some signs."

"Just one: Do not touch."

"Well, we need more storage space," Deena said.

"You say that every day," Kathy said. "But you never have time to work on that old chest in the garage."

"That chest is too ugly ever to be beautiful," Deena said. "Trust me. I know about these things."

Truce or no truce, Kathy wasn't going to just go along with everything Queen Deena said.

This one ended in a long staring match.

* * *

But during the following week the town of Cranford saw something it had never seen before: the Cranberry Cousins getting along and hanging out together—mostly at McGowan's Bakery. They began stopping there every morning on their way to school. They had both developed what Deena called "a strong affinity" and Kathy called an "awesome craving" for McGowan's warm apple fritters. Kathy found herself sketching fritters on quiz papers. Deena wrote about them in her journal, describing how, since she discovered them, her life had been enriched.

"Good morning, A.J.," Deena said when she and Kathy walked into the bakery one crisp Wednesday morning.

"Good morning, C.C.'s," said A.J. to the two girls. Alice June McGowan, who preferred A.J., was a short, round woman with red hair that was always pinned back in a bun entirely appropriate for a baker.

"Two apple fritters," Kathy said, leaning on the glass display case and feeling the warmth of the fresh-baked goodies.

"And orange juice, please," said Deena.

"Two a.f.'s and two o.j.'s," said A.J. "A.S.A.P."

"I could live here," Kathy said.

"You practically do," Deena said.

A.J. brought the hot fritters on paper plates and the orange juice in Styrofoam cups and set them on the counter. After paying for the food, the two girls stood off to one side of the bakery, enjoying their breakfast.

"Want a job?" A.J. asked in between customers.

"Tasting?" Kathy said.

"Sweeping up after school, keeping the store neat," said A.J.

Deena laughed.

"Can't after school," Kathy said.

"Too busy avoiding her jobs at the inn every day," Deena said.

"Well, *I* get all the hard jobs," Kathy said to Deena.

"How's the old inn coming, anyway?" asked A.J.

"Only half the rooms are ready," Deena said.

The door opened, and the girls watched as a guy walked into the bakery. As soon as she saw him, Deena gave Kathy a nudge—practically plunging her elbow all the way through Kathy's ribs.

"That's him," Deena whispered. "That's the guy I saw the first day of school."

"Hi, A.J.," he said, looking at Kathy and smiling at Deena. "Got any cranberry muffins?"

Deena and Kathy kept eating their apple fritters—very slowly. "Should I do something?" Deena whispered.

"Like what? Pay for his cranberry muffin?" Kathy said. "He's a total geek. Forget it."

"When's the last time you had your vision checked?" Deena asked.

The boy paid for his muffin and left, saying, "See you later, cousins."

"Who is that, A.J.?" Deena asked.

"Ken Buckly," A.J. said, brushing powdered sugar off her apron. "He's on the ski team."

"Interesting," Deena said. "*Intensely* interesting. Does he live in town or out in the country? I wonder."

"In town," A.J. said. "His parents own the lumber store, and they put up that sign on Route twenty-four. The one that says 'Cranford wasn't built in a day.' City council argued for three weeks about whether or not to take it down," A.J. said, laughing.

"Does he have a job?" Deena asked. "And does he have a car? Is he going with anyone?"

"You don't happen to know his I.Q., do you, A.J.?" Kathy added teasingly.

A.J. laughed and shook her head. "You've just read my whole file on Ken Buckly," she told Deena.

A minute later a man walked into the bakery. It was Mr. Millander, the American history teacher. Besides being the teacher with the toughest reputation in school, he was also the tallest teacher and the only one who wore a red plaid hunting hat with the flaps pulled down over his ears.

"You're late this morning, Brad," A.J. said, pouring a cup of coffee as soon as he walked in.

"Car broke down," Mr. Millander said. He looked over at the Cranberry Cousins. "You girls are late for homeroom," Mr. Millander added.

Deena practically spit her orange juice. "Late? I can't be late," she said. "My mom will have kittens!"

"We've already got enough kittens," Kathy said. She watched Mr. Millander staring at her.

Well, this is it, Kathy thought. Mr. Millander's big chance to get even with me for passing out gum in his class.

"O.K., we're late. What's the difference?" Kathy said.

Mr. Millander took a slow sip of his coffee and shook his head. "I've seen a lot of students like you, Manelli," he said. "There's always one—you don't play by the rules and you don't join the team. But you could be one heck of a player!"

Kathy held very still, waiting for the ax to fall.

Mr. Millander put his cup on the counter. "See you tomorrow, A.J.," he said. Before he left, he took several pads of printed forms from his coat pocket. He wrote out two slips and gave them to Kathy and Deena.

"These are late passes," Deena said.

"What do you know? Looks like I brought enough for everyone,"Mr. Millander said, smiling on his way out.

After he was gone, Deena collected her books but lost her composure. "I can't believe it," she said. "He actually gave us excuses."

Kathy hid her own surprise behind a shrug. "How about another apple fritter, now that we've got the excuses?" she said with a sly smile.

Deena let out an exasperated sigh and practically dragged Kathy to school.

The halls were empty when they got there. Classes had begun. As they put their things in their lockers, Deena said, "See you after school."

"I won't be home," Kathy said.

"Where do you go every day?" Deena asked.

Kathy closed her locker. "See ya," she said.

* * *

The truce was definitely working out, Kathy decided happily as she watched Deena doing her homework a few nights later. Ever since the two of them had stopped fighting, their mothers had been getting along better, too. Kathy's mother hadn't said word one about moving back to San Francisco. Who knows—maybe she called the West Coast and found out nobody was home for her, either. Whatever the reason, Kathy was glad they were staying in Cranford and *totally* glad that World War Three had come to an end.

She looked over at Deena and squinted her eyes. More purple, Kathy decided. While Deena was hard at work on an oral report for Mrs. Godfrey's English class, Kathy was working on Deena . . . in a way. She was lying on her bed holding a framed portrait of Deena and drawing on the glass with different-colored grease pencils—trying outrageous eye make-ups on Deena. Each time she had a good one, she'd interrupt Deena's concentration to show her the photo.

"Are you kidding?" Deena said, recoiling at the sight. "I couldn't show my face except on Ground Hog Day."

"Come on," Kathy said, putting the photo on Deena's desk. "The idea is, you make a statement with your face."

"My face *does* make a statement," Deena said, pulling her hair back so that her cheekbones would show. "My face says, 'Hello. I'm Deena Scott, an intelligent and worthy human being.' This face, however—"she handed the photo back to Kathy—"this face says, 'Hello. I've been dead for fifty years and I want to drink your blood.' "

Kathy wiped the grease pencil off the photo and went back to creating her cousin's new image. Meanwhile, two of the kittens played pounce with Kathy's toes at the foot of her bed.

"Deena!"

Footsteps pounded up the stairs from the second floor and invaded the cousins' room. It was Deena's mom, Lydia, followed closely by Nancy. Both of them were carrying rolls of wallpaper under their arms, and the two sisters were giggling.

"Deena, don't listen to her," Nancy said, pushing ahead.

"You're trying to influence the judge. Shameful. Shameful," Lydia said. "Deena, Deena, Deena, darling, we need your opinion. Guest room number five. Very sunny, right? Windows on the east, windows on the south. I think we should use this wallpaper. What do you think?" Lydia unrolled a large bright flowered print.

"Absolutely wrong," Nancy said. "No taste. Your mother must eat the kitten chow for a midnight snack."

"You overgrown hippie, what do you know?" Lydia said, teasing her sister. "Besides, I only eat it for breakfast."

Nancy giggled as she unrolled her wallpaper sample, a geometric pattern of shaded lines.

"No," Lydia said. "People come here to have fun—not read a will. But what do you think, Dee?"

Kathy watched as Deena looked from one wallpaper to the other, and then from one sister to the other. The two women waited expectantly for Deena's decision. No one looked at Kathy. Not Deena . . . not Lydia . . . not even Kathy's own mom. They couldn't care less what she thought.

"I can't tell," Deena said.

"Deena Scott," said Lydia. "I didn't raise you to be indecisive."

"Mom, I can't tell up here. We've got to take the samples into the room," Deena said. "Wallpaper is not just about colors. It's about space and visual openness."

"I thought it was just about paste and killing your back putting it up," Nancy said, rolling up her sample.

"Of course, you're right, Deena," Lydia said, rolling up her wallpaper. "Come on."

Without even a glance in Kathy's direction, Deena, her mother, and her aunt left the room.

"Well, since I'm not here," Kathy said, "they can't complain about my music being too loud."

She turned on a tape full blast and almost slammed the door to her room. But she stopped herself.

The thing was, it really hurt to be ignored, because, whether they knew it or not, Kathy had lots of ideas about the guest rooms. Comfortable chairs closer to the window—a skier's dream. Guest room number five was one of her favorites. Its walls met in many angles. Both wallpapers were totally wrong for a room that said "I'm not like any other room in the house."

Besides, Kathy thought, just because she hadn't done that much work around the inn, it didn't mean she wasn't interested. Anyway, they could have at least asked her which wallpaper she liked just to be polite! Well, who cares!

Kathy finally decided on just the right make-up for Deena. She took a black grease pencil and made two huge dark circles around Deena's eyes. Then she blacked out a couple of her teeth and finally gave her a large, black mustache.

There, perfect, Kathy thought with a laugh.

Chapter 8

Mornings and evenings were truce time. But after school was Kathy's time—time to wander around through the neighborhoods of Cranford, looking for a garage band. Every day, when Kathy's mom asked, "Where have you been, Kath?" she'd say, "Just walking, Mom." She said it to drive Deena crazy, but it was also the truth. She was walking—walking through neighborhoods where people lived in normal small houses instead of inns.

Whenever she heard a band practicing, she'd stop and check them out. She could tell in an instant if they were any good. They had to have that special combination of sounds—and that special collision of egos—that go into a great band. That was the kind of band Kathy wanted to join.

She was also listening for a different sound—the sound of a motorcycle. Roy's motorcycle. He seemed to disappear every day after school. And his friends, like Ellecia and Zee, didn't know where he went.

What Kathy wanted more than anything was for Roy to pass her on his cycle, see her, screech to a stop, and talk for a while. O.K., she'd even settle for a gradual stop and forget the tire skids. But would he stop for her? *That* was the question. She hadn't gotten a good look at his bike, but she was pretty sure it didn't have a bumper sticker that said "I brake for girls."

On Friday afternoon, one week before the Bexley Bonfire, Kathy walked for an extra long time, once again without running into Roy. It was almost dusk by the time she wandered into the kitchen and said hi to her mom.

"Kath, I thought you and I were going to polish the brass lamps this afternoon."

"I totally forgot, Mom," Kathy said, glancing quickly at Deena, who was standing by the refrigerator.

"Where were you?" Nancy asked.

"Just walking, Mom."

Deena was nibbling on a carrot, but she took a sudden chomp that sounded like it could crack an incisor.

Then Lydia walked into the kitchen, her face smudged with dirt and her hair tied back with a kerchief. "I am exhausted," she said.

"I'm sort of halfway between spaced-out and dead," Nancy said. "I never thought this inn was so big when I was a kid."

"Everything gets bigger when you have to clean it," Lydia said, drinking from a jar of cranberry juice.

"Please don't say that in front of Kathy," Deena said.

"Why don't you girls make dinner tonight?" Lydia said.

"Great idea," Nancy said.

"Mom, you know me: I'd love to make macaroni and cheese for you just once more before I die," Kathy said, "but Deena and I are going out for a pizza."

Come on, Deena. Don't look so surprised or you'll blow this whole plan.

"Yeah, you know, it's been a week. No fights, no screaming, no blood," Kathy continued. "So we're going to go share a little double anchovies."

"*Double* anchovies?" Deena said, but then she held her tongue.

"Well, I think it's great," Nancy said before Lydia had a chance to object. "We've noticed how much better you two have been getting along."

Kathy smiled.

* * *

On Friday and Saturday night, after seven o'clock, no adult in Cranford ate in the Pizza Hut. It was common knowledge that teenagers moved in and took over. So when Kathy and Deena got there, the place was packed. And the scene looked like a game of musical chairs. Kids moved chairs from table to table to sit and talk with their friends for a few minutes and then move on to another table.

Deena was wearing a pale, hand-knit fisherman's sweater and a light brown straight skirt. And Kathy was wearing black pants with wide imitation snakeskin suspenders over a purple T-shirt and a 1950s-style man's jacket. They both wanted to make an impression on the crowd, not realizing that the biggest impression they made was by showing up together.

"Kathy!" a high-pitched but raspy voice called. It could only be Ellecia.

Kathy spotted Ellecia waving to her from a table. She was sitting with Zee, a couple of other guys—and Roy! Kathy's heart skipped a beat.

"There are no tables," she said, pulling Deena's arm. "Let's sit over here."

"What about the table in the corner? It's empty," Deena said, surprised at being jerked in the opposite direction.

"The waitress has lice," Kathy said. She knew that was enough to make Deena insist on sitting at least two states away. Kathy steered her cousin over to Ellecia's table, and she made Zee move over so Deena was sitting between Zee and Ellecia. That way Kathy wound up next to Roy.

Zee looked at Deena and said, "Everybody put on your sunglasses. The two-hundred-watt bulb is here."

"How's it going, Roy?" Kathy asked.

"How's what going?" Roy asked with concern.

"I don't know," Kathy said. "Your life, your pizza, your investments—whatever."

Roy smiled. "It's going O.K. I've been thinking of getting new tires for my bike," he said.

"This is getting too metaphysical for me," Deena mumbled. But Kathy had forgotten that her cousin was even there. She and Roy started talking with Kelvin and Gregg, who went to the neighboring Bexley High School. They were all making plans for the big bonfire.

After a while, Ellecia plopped a large wad of gum from her mouth onto the top of her silver skull ring so she could take a bite of pizza. "Hey, I heard your essay on that poem, 'The Waist Line,'" she said to Deena.

"'The Waste Land,'" Deena corrected, staring at Ellecia's skull ring.

"Whatever," said Ellecia with a shake of her black hair. Her bright blue forelock fell into her face.

"But you're not in our class," Deena said.

"Mrs. Godfrey read it to us," Ellecia said.

"Well," Deena said, smiling, "what did you think of it?"

"I didn't get it," Ellecia said. "You wrote so much."

"Thank you," said Deena. "But what part didn't you get?"

"How you could write so much," Zee said.

Every time Zee got in a zinger, she and Ellecia would give each other a quick high-five.

It didn't get much better after that. Everyone at the table seemed to agree about the same things—except Deena. Deena didn't think school was a major waste of time, she never faked hiccups in class to get out of a quiz, and she couldn't imagine asking Nuclear Waste to write a new national anthem.

"And they should get Kathy to record it," Ellecia said. "She's mind-blowing."

"Yeah, but I knew that when you sang in the stairwell," Roy said with a smile.

The evening could have ended right there as far as Kathy was concerned.

"She does have a good voice," Deena said. "But it's hard to know how good until you sing some real songs, Kath."

"Nuclear Waste doesn't write real songs?" Kathy asked.

"Come on, Kathy," Deena said, shaking her head. "'Driving down the roads, running over toads'—what kind of a song is that? It has such a mock sense of tragedy. It's not even written from a clear point of view."

"What would you like? A song written from the toad's point of view?" Zee answered.

Now that she was paying attention to the real world again, Kathy saw how tense the table was, and she knew the reason, too—Deena. "Enough, O.K., Deena?" Kathy said, trying to stop things right there.

"This heavy metal music," Deena said, ignoring Kathy's hint. "Honestly, it just doesn't make musical sense."

"This should be good," Zee said.

"What does it say?" Deena asked. "It says: We don't know what's going on and we don't care. Obviously the only people who like it have very little self-esteem."

"I'm so ashamed of myself," Zee said, bursting into fake tears.

"I'm going to go brush my hair," Deena said, standing up. "Could you and I talk, Kathy?"

"In a minute," Kathy said.

"It's very important," Deena said before she left.

Everyone watched her walk off to the bathroom.

"Why hasn't someone made a doll out of her?" Ellecia said.

"Hey, look, you guys, lighten up," Kathy said. She could see Ellecia and Zee were surprised at this change of heart. "We've been getting along, O.K.? She's not a bad kid," Kathy said. "You like her some, don't you, Roy?"

Roy slid his mirror sunglasses down on his nose and looked over them at Kathy. "Is this a test?" he asked.

* * *

Deena's brush tore at her hair in angry strokes as she looked at herself in the bathroom mirror. What was she doing here? she asked herself. What on earth could have possessed her to trust her cousin this far?

Let's go out for a pizza, Kathy says. And then she spends the whole time talking to a jerk who's about as smart as a telephone booth, while her friends sit there eating a revolting combination pizza and cutting me into slices. She only came here to get out of making dinner anyway, Deena thought. Or maybe she was just using me as an excuse to meet Roy here.

Whatever her reasons, they obviously didn't include

spending time with me, Deena realized. In short, a typical evening with Kathy Manelli.

When Deena came back to the table, it was noise as usual in the restaurant but strangely quiet at the table. Everyone was looking at her. Probably because they've never seen smooth, brushed hair that lies flat, Deena thought to herself.

"Deena!" Kathy blurted out just as Deena sat down.

She sat down fast and hard, but she seemed to slide around on the chair. There was something soft and wet on her chair.

Everyone was trying not to laugh but not doing a very good job of it.

Deena stood up and looked at her chair. A piece of pizza was smashed on the seat and she knew just where the rest of it was—squashed all over the back of her skirt. Deena looked at Kathy, who was trying to avoid Deena's eyes.

"How could you do this?" Deena shouted, her face as red as the tomato sauce on her skirt.

"I didn't do anything," Kathy said.

"You didn't stop it," Deena said.

"It was a joke," Zee said.

"No, a joke is why did the chicken cross the road," Deena said. Tears welled up in her eyes. "A joke is when you say something in class and everyone except the teacher laughs. But you wouldn't know a joke, or anything else, if it hit you in the face!" She flicked off a glob of tomato sauce from her hand and it landed on Zee's face.

The restaurant suddenly became a theater and Deena was on stage.

"This is unforgivable," she declared to Kathy. "And it's exactly what I deserve for ever, *ever* thinking that someone like you could be trusted."

Then Deena stormed out of the restaurant, covered not only in pizza but also humiliation.

It was a long walk home from the Pizza Hut on a very chilly night. But the biggest ache was inside Deena's heart. No one, in her entire life, had ever treated Deena as badly as Kathy had—or hurt her as much. And the worst part was that she had gone along with it, set herself up for it even. She had willingly walked in there with Kathy, just to be dumped the minute Kathy spotted her *real* friends.

Well, no more, Deena thought to herself. Never again would Kathy Manelli get close enough to tamper with the inner workings of Deena Scott's soul.

As Deena walked uphill through the cold and windy night, a motorcycle zipped past her on the road. The people on the bike didn't see Deena, but she saw them. And it made her even angrier. It was Roy, with Kathy sitting behind him, her arms wrapped tightly around his waist. Perfect, just perfect, Deena thought. She's not supposed to ride on that motorcycle. But Kathy wouldn't let something like the rules stop her. Nothing stops her from doing anything she wants, anytime she wants—to anyone!

Chapter 9

By the time Deena walked in the front door of the Cranberry Inn, she was walking stiffly because of the cold. She headed straight for the stairs, but her mother looked up from the registration desk she was sanding and stopped her.

"Hi, Mom," Deena said.

"Have a good time?"

"Mother, I can honestly say I will never forget tonight," Deena said. She thought she was doing a remarkable job of controlling her voice.

"Well, it must have been some pizza," Lydia said.

Deena was surprised her mother couldn't smell it. "It was unlike any I've ever had before," she said.

"Nancy, Johnny, and I ended up splitting a can of tuna fish with the kittens."

"I hope you don't mean you all ate out of the can," Deena said. She could even tell jokes. She was going to make it. It was touch and go for a while, but she was going to pull through—if she could just get upstairs and take off her skirt and tear it into a million pieces, burn the pieces, and then find a new school to go to and a new town to live in.

Deena began to back slowly away from her mother and toward the stairs.

"Deena, where's Kathy?"

As far as Deena was concerned, Kathy was dead. She had passed over from the living world the moment she joined in the conspiracy to replace her seat cushion with a slice of sausage and guacamole pizza. But Deena didn't say any of that out loud. She just shrugged and kept walking.

"Deena, didn't you hear me? I asked where's Kathy? Isn't she with you?"

"No, she's not with me. Trust your eyes, Mother. You can see for yourself Kathy isn't with me."

"Deena," Lydia said icily, "I do not expect to be treated this way."

"Nobody expects it, Mother."

"Deena, you can turn that tone of voice off right now. You are not Kathy. And I am not your Aunt Nancy. *We* make rules and we stick to them in this family. Now you

94

girls may be fifteen years old, but that's not old enough for either of you to be walking home at *this* hour by yourselves."

"Mother!" Deena shouted at a volume which surprised both of them. She turned her back to her mother. "I am wearing a pizza! Everyone in the entire school has seen me. In one month—because of your idea to move here—I have been reduced from Deena Scott to a Cranberry Cousin and from now on I'll probably be known as the Pizza Queen! Get off my case!!!"

Deena bolted up the stairs and slammed the door to her room behind her. She fell onto her bed, almost landing on three very startled, snoozing kittens that were cuddling together. She began crying softly into her pillow.

Her mother knocked on the door. "Deena," she said.

"The door's closed, Mother, and we have rules about respecting privacy when the door is closed, don't we?" Deena said.

"I want to talk to you, sweetheart."

Lydia opened the door and moved Deena's desk chair over to the bed so she could sit near her.

"What happened?"

"I hate her," Deena said. "She dragged me over to sit with her friends, and it was like talking to earthworms. They didn't understand a word I said, and they couldn't care less. Then, when I went to the restroom, they put pizza on my chair."

Nancy had followed her sister upstairs, and now she came to the doorway, eating an ice cream sandwich. "I heard the door slam and thought Kathy was home," she

95

said with a laugh. "Am I breaking and entering a family situation?"

"Kathy's not home," Lydia said. "Deena left without her."

"But, Mother," Deena said before she started to cry again.

"Oh, don't worry about Kathy," Nancy said. "I'm sure she can take care of herself."

"You can say that again," Deena said.

"That's not the point," Lydia said, putting a hand on her daughter. "Sweetheart, I'm very sorry about what happened, and I can see you have a good reason to be angry with Kathy. But I expected the two of you to come home together tonight."

Deena couldn't believe what was happening. She had just come home from the most humiliating night of her life, and her mother was blaming her for everything. Once again the Kathy Manelli luck ran true to form. She could ignore her responsibilities, she could trick people, she could use them, and she could get away with it. It wasn't fair!

"I'm the one whose skirt is covered in pizza. I didn't do anything wrong!" Deena cried. "I didn't just sit there while my friends were terrible to my cousin."

"But you left your cousin halfway across town in the middle of the night. How is she supposed to get home?" Lydia said.

"She could *walk*, like I did," Deena said angrily. "But I'm sure she won't have to. I'm sure *Roy* will bring her home whenever she wants him to."

"She was with Roy?" Nancy asked. Suddenly she had that sound in her voice. It was the sound all parents got when they were hot on the trail of their kids disobeying them.

"Well, yes, Roy was at the Pizza Hut," Deena said. She got off the bed and walked to the window. She stared out at the street so she wouldn't have to look at her aunt. There was a terrible knot forming in her stomach, like she was doing something very wrong. But she wasn't sure what it was.

"So what exactly do you mean, Roy will bring her home?" Nancy asked. "Did she go off with him on that motorcycle?"

"Deena, turn around. Tell us the truth," Lydia said.

"You know I don't lie, Mother," Deena said. She had never lied to her mother and she wasn't going to start now. "Yeah, when I was walking home, I saw them together."

"On the motorcycle?" Nancy asked again, just to make sure.

"*Yes*," Deena said.

"Well, that's it," Nancy said. "I've had it with her."

Deena didn't know whether to be glad that Kathy was finally in deep trouble—or feel guilty for being the cause of it.

"Did you change your mind about allowing her to ride on that boy's motorcycle?" Lydia asked her sister.

"No—I *told* her she couldn't!" Nancy said, really raising her voice for the first time.

Deena was beginning to feel sick to her stomach. Could it possibly be true that Kathy Manelli was finally going

97

to get what was coming to her? She deserved it, Deena thought. But then, why did she feel so bad?

* * *

The wind blew across Kathy's face as she and Roy sped through the starry night, touring Cranford. Kathy was loving every second of her ride. She loved her arms around Roy's waist and the feel of his leather jacket, the occasional autumn leaf in her face, and even the cold wind that stung her cheeks. Roy showed her all the roads and back roads of the town, and they cruised the village square a couple of times. Finally they ended the tour driving into Cranford Park. Roy turned off the engine and the headlight, and got off the bike.

"What a great ride," Kathy said. Her head was warm from wearing the cycle helmet, but her face was cold. Roy put his hands on her cheeks and pretended to shiver.

"This is Cranford Park. Most of the jerks at school think this is a great place to drink and throw up. So I come here late, when they've all gone," he said.

They listened and heard nothing but the wind through the thick trees. They walked until they were in the woods, surrounded by pine trees and stepping on a carpet of soft needles. Roy picked up pine cones and tried to juggle them. Then Kathy tried. Neither of them was very good at it.

"How's your face? Still frozen?"

"A little," she said.

Roy put his hands on her cheeks again and held them

there a long time. Finally she pulled his arm down, and they walked farther into the park, holding hands.

"We had a great park in San Francisco," Kathy said. "Golden Gate Park. It had everything. Even buffalo."

"I wonder," Roy said.

"What?"

"My cousin says he punched a buffalo once. Wonder what that felt like," Roy said. "Hey, did you . . . "

"Did I punch a buffalo?" Kathy asked, laughing.

"No. Did you go with anyone?" he asked.

"No," Kathy said. "We just hung out. What about you?"

"What do you think?"

"I think it's your turn to answer," she said.

"Hey, girls come and go, you know," he said with a grin. "Mostly go."

Kathy didn't know how to take that. She looked away.

"Hey, sometimes there are reasons, you know?" Roy said.

Kathy wished Roy would keep talking. After fifteen years, she was finally having a totally perfect day. And if they kept talking, she wouldn't have to think about having to go back to the inn. But Roy got quiet again. Still, Kathy could tell something was on his mind.

"What are you thinking?" she asked.

"About you," he said. After a minute he reached into his jacket and pulled out a wooden match. He looked at it for a second and then struck it against the zipper of his jacket. The match flamed and made their faces orange for a moment. "That's you," he said. "They used to make these matches here in Cranford. They're not safety matches. They'll light up on anything."

They watched the match burn all the way down to Roy's fingertips. Kathy blew it out at the last second.

Kathy sat down on a picnic table, and Roy sat on the bench. She reached into his jacket and took out another one of the old-fashioned matches. She struck it with her long fingernail and watched it burn down to her fingertips. Roy blew it out at the last second.

"My dad used to work at the old match factory," he said.

"Used to?"

"It's history."

"Don't tell me it burned down," Kathy said.

"Yeah, it really did," Roy said.

"Someone smoking on the job?" Kathy asked.

"Lightning hit it!"

They both laughed.

Suddenly Roy stood up, put his hands on her face, and kissed her.

A car horn blew several long blasts.

"What's that?"

"Car horn," he explained. "That's the park ranger in the parking lot. He sees my bike and he's saying the park's closing."

So they started to walk back. Roy took her hand again. "The Bexley Bonfire. What about you?" he said.

"Yeah, I decided I might as well go," Kathy said.

"What about me?"

What was he saying? Was he asking her to go with him?

"Yeah—you should go," Kathy said, playing it safe.

"What I mean is, do you want to go with me?"

He finally said the words!

"Yeah, that would be great," Kathy said, beaming at him.

She was smiling so hard, her face hurt.

During the ride home, she tried to remember everything that happened. She could still feel the kiss.

"This is the way I'm thinking about it!" Roy shouted above the engine noise as they rode through the streets. "I'm definitely going to be the one who finds the Bexley Lion this year."

"How do you know?" Kathy yelled.

"Fastest bike, two heads, four eyes, and great gas mileage," Roy laughed. "We'll cover all of Bexley, you and me."

"Sounds unbeatable," Kathy said, hugging Roy's shoulder.

When they were a few blocks from the Cranberry Inn, Kathy tapped Roy and told him to stop.

"My mom said I'm not allowed to ride with you," Kathy said. "So you'd better let me off here. But don't worry. I've got a week to work on her. I know after I talk to her, it'll be O.K."

"Yeah. Work it out," Roy said. "Cause I know I won't find the lion without you."

"I'm going in right now and talk to her," Kathy said.

"Tell her I got an extra helmet," Roy said as Kathy handed hers back to him.

"Right," Kathy smiled. "She's no problem. Really. See you later."

"Good luck," Roy called to her. And then he drove off.

Kathy ran the rest of the way to the inn. Maybe she'd have to wake her mom up. But that was O.K. She couldn't possibly wait till morning to talk to her.

Chapter 10

With a large harvest moon smiling brightly behind her, Kathy rushed into the Cranberry Inn, hoping to talk to her mother. But as soon as she entered the huge front room, she knew something was wrong. All the lights were out except for a glowing fire in the fireplace, and her mother was waiting up for her. Nancy was sitting in the large soft leather chair she had brought from California and looking into the flickering logs.

"Hey, you're awake. That's great," Kathy said, walking over to the fireplace. "I've got to talk to you."

"Did you have a nice motorcycle ride?" Nancy asked coldly.

Kathy's heart started pounding; she didn't know what to say. Her mom looked very bent out of shape.

"How did you know?" Kathy asked. But she didn't have to wait for an answer. There was only one person who would get a major thrill out of spying on Kathy and then rushing home to tell everyone what a bad girl she had been. Sweet Deena!

"Mom, I was going to tell you," Kathy said.

"I'm sure," Nancy said. "You've had a big day, haven't you? You 'forgot' to show up to work on the inn. You embarrassed your cousin in front of half the school, and then you finished the night off by disobeying my rule about riding with Roy."

"But, Mom—I thought it would be okay. He got another helmet."

"Well, it's not okay!" Nancy said loudly. "You should have asked me first, do you understand?"

"You sound just like Aunt Lydia," Kathy said. "Since when do *you* make a big deal about rules?"

"Oh, so my rules don't count now? Your Aunt Lydia was right. You have absolutely no respect for what I say."

"Mom, you know that isn't true." Kathy was desperate.

"Did I say you couldn't ride the motorcycle or didn't I?" her mother asked, flipping her hair away from her face with her hand.

"It was a dumb rule, and you know it," Kathy said.

"I didn't ask for your judicial opinion," Nancy said. "You were expected to do what I told you. Now, you're not allowed to ride on *anyone's* motorcycle. And you are not allowed to go out with that boy, Roy, at all. I *forbid* you to see him, Kathy. I think we need to establish some rules around here."

"Mom," Kathy pleaded. "You're not being fair. You're not even *listening* to me!"

"Now you understand how *I* feel most of the time," Nancy said.

"No. You can't do that!" Kathy cried angrily.

"Oh, can't I? Just watch me!" Nancy said.

Kathy practically flew up the stairs to her room and banged the door open loudly as if she needed to get Deena's attention. Deena was sitting in bed reading a book. She didn't look up when Kathy started slamming things around the room. Finally Kathy took the direct approach.

"Deena!" she demanded. "How *could* you tell my mom about Roy?"

"I'm not talking or listening to you—ever again," Deena said.

"What did you do? Write an essay about the dangers of motorcycles and give it to my mom?" Kathy shouted.

"You wouldn't understand."

Kathy laughed. "You bet I don't understand," she said. "Hey—did you get all the facts and all the dates and all the references right? Because I know you like to be perfect and right. Always right. We rode all over Cranford together. Everyone saw us—there are a million witnesses. And then we went to Cranford Park. It was fabulous. He talked and made jokes. And then he kissed me and asked me to go to the Bexley Bonfire with him. Are you underlining all this in your notes? And I was coming in to tell my mom all about it—but it was too late. You had already handed in your homework."

"Poor you," Deena snapped. "Everything happens to you. You're always the victim. Nothing ever happens to anyone else." Deena jumped off her bed and threw her pizza-stained skirt at Kathy's feet. "Did everyone get a big laugh tonight?"

"A lot of people liked it, yeah. Some people get tired of you knowing everything and telling everyone what to think."

"I don't tell anyone what to think," Deena said, throwing her book on the bed. "I challenge them to think—and with your friends, that's an enormous challenge."

"You don't know anything about my friends!"

"And I plan to make that a habit," Deena said. "You're incredible. You said we were going for a pizza just so you could get out of cooking tonight. That made me feel really great for starters. Then the minute you saw that group in the Pizza Hut, you dumped me."

"Oh, sorry. Maybe I should have a pizza with your friends sometime. They'd probably make me take a quiz at the end. And it wasn't just because I saw my friends. Roy was there," Kathy said, trying to explain. She had to tell someone about him. "Don't you understand, Deena? I really like him. I've been trying to talk to him all week."

"Haven't you ever heard of the telephone?"

"You're so smart, you know everything. Tell me, who do I call to have you taken away?" Kathy said.

"Just keep shouting," Deena said. "If you make enough noise, I'm sure your mother will go back to San Francisco."

"Oh, sure!" Kathy shouted. "That would make your mother happy. Then maybe your mother will get a *divorce* from my mother. But you know all about that, don't you?"

Deena's eyes were tearing up, but Kathy didn't care. She had never been so furious in her life.

"Don't you ever cross this line," Deena said, drawing an imaginary line down the middle of the room.

Kathy charged across the line and pulled some books out of Deena's bookcase like a child. They scattered on the floor.

"My journals! Are you crazy?" Deena cried, running and grabbing her books into her arms.

"Yes, I'm crazy!" Kathy shouted. "How would you feel? *She won't ever let me see Roy again!* You've ruined everything!"

Deena was kneeling over her journals, but when she heard that, she sat down. "I never thought that would happen," she said in a quiet voice.

"I know. It's better than you hoped for, isn't it?"

Kathy started dialing a telephone number.

"What are you doing?"

"Haven't you ever heard of the telephone?" Kathy asked. Ellecia answered at the other end.

"Hello," Ellecia croaked.

"Ellecia, it's Kathy. Can I stay with you tonight?"

"Hey, Kath, Zee is sleeping over. I'm booked up," Ellecia said.

Kathy hung up without saying anything else and started stuffing her clothes into a laundry bag.

"Where are you going?" Deena asked.

"I'm not staying in this room with you another minute!" Kathy cried. She pulled the drawstring on the laundry bag and opened the door.

"But where are you going?"

Kathy didn't answer. She dragged her bag of clothes to the top of the stairs and then gave it a kick. It rolled, bumped, and thumped all the way down.

"What's going on?" Nancy called from her bedroom.

"Leave me alone!" Kathy shouted back. "Just everyone leave me completely alone!"

On the second floor Kathy looked into one of the guest rooms, and for a minute she thought of sleeping there. But the beds had no mattresses, and most of the rooms were halfway between being painted or wallpapered.

So instead she went to a storage closet and began tossing things out until she found what she needed—Johnny's camping tent. She dragged that and a sleeping bag, plus her clothes into the back yard.

For the next twenty minutes Kathy tried in vain to set up the tent, but it kept collapsing. It didn't matter though—she didn't really want to be warm. She wanted to be furious and cold and miserable, so everyone would realize how they had completely and totally ruined her life.

"Nobody's going to tell me what to do anymore," Kathy said out loud. Then she realized she was talking to the orange-striped mother cat. The cat had left her babies in the attic to check out the sounds in the back yard. "I'm going to be like you. Come and go when I want. I won't get off chairs or move just because someone tells me to."

The cat meowed happily and rubbed against Kathy's leg.

"No, dummy," Kathy said, picking up the cat and petting it. "Don't ask anyone to be nice to you. Don't let them know that's what you want. That's when they step on your paws or pull your whiskers out or something."

"Kathy!" Deena called, coming out of the back door.

What's she doing here? She probably spent twenty minutes picking out the right robe to go with the nightgown.

"What are you doing?" Deena asked.

"Trying for a merit badge," Kathy snapped. "Leave me alone."

"You can't stay out here all night," Deena said. She was wrapped in a blanket and pulled it tighter around her. "It's freezing."

"Just watch me!" Kathy said. She threw down the tent poles and climbed into the sleeping bag, trying to get warm.

She could see that Deena was already shivering from the cold. She can't take the heat and she can't take the cold, Kathy thought to herself. She's pitiful.

"Kathy, you don't understand. I didn't mean to rat on you."

Kathy didn't say anything.

"Haven't you ever been sorry just a little too late?" Deena asked.

"I'm asleep," Kathy said.

"O.K., fine. Stay out here. I know how much you enjoy being a stubborn and stupid jerk."

"Go sit on a pizza," Kathy said.

"Why are you being so dumb?" Deena said. "It's freezing out here."

"Roy is the most fabulous guy who ever kissed me," Kathy said. "And you ruined everything!"

Deena took off the blanket she was wearing and threw it on Kathy. Then she ran back inside.

That night Deena didn't get much sleep. The room seemed large, lonely, and full of shadows. And no matter how many blankets she piled on her bed, she couldn't seem to get warm. She rolled and twisted in her bedcovers, and then finally she got out of bed to look out the window on the stairway landing. From there she could see into the back yard, where Kathy was camping. But it was too dark to see whether Kathy was still there . . . too dark to go back outside and apologize . . . .

"I'll never, never rat on anyone again," Deena said softly as she looked up into the starless night.

Chapter 11

When Kathy woke up the next morning, the sun was up and the air was unusually warm. It was an Indian summer kind of day—warm for late September—and it made the fighting and screaming from last night seem very far away.

Kathy stood up, stiff and sore from sleeping on the ground, and began to gather up all the gear.

What time was it anyway?

Should she go in and have it out with her mother? Wouldn't her mother give in, especially when Kathy explained it to her? After all—Kathy and her mom were a lot alike. Which meant her mom liked to throw a good tantrum once in a while, too. But she always got over them.

But last night was different—totally different from anything before.

If she went into the inn, she didn't know what her mother would say today. She knew what Johnny would say. "You took my tent without asking." And Deena—well, she was the absolute last person Kathy ever wanted to see again.

So instead of going in, Kathy took a walk, one of her long quiet walks to the other side of Cranford, as close to the other side of the world as she could get.

Kids were playing in piles of leaves, drivers were adding antifreeze to their cars, teenagers hung around in groups. Everyone else was acting like it was just another day.

As Kathy passed a flat red brick house with the garage door slightly open, all of a sudden an awesome sound exploded from inside the garage. Three guitars and two drums were making a sound that shook leaves from the trees. Kathy couldn't move. She was feeling a million different things at once. Unbelievable! She wasn't even looking for a band today, but she knew instantly that this was a real group!

When the song was over, the garage door opened all the way and Kathy could see the five guys inside. They all had long hair, silver earrings, and banged-up instruments. Both drummers had skulls painted on their bass drums with the name, The Fury.

Kathy recognized a couple of them from her classes. But she didn't know their names.

When the band started to play again, Kathy sat down on the hood of an old Camaro parked in front of the house and listened. She knew the music. It was Nuclear Waste from one of their first albums. But something wasn't clicking right.

Suddenly the band just stopped.

"Hey!" the lead guitarist shouted angrily at Kathy. He was tall and blond and kept the sleeves of his T-shirt rolled up high. "We don't want an audience, O.K.?"

Kathy slid off the car and walked slowly toward the garage, zipping up her wide-shouldered black leather jacket. "Hey, you know the notes, but that doesn't mean you're playing the music," she said.

The five guys looked at each other and laughed a little. "Yeah? What's wrong with it?" asked one of the drummers, who had a black patch over one eye. He lifted the patch to get a better look at Kathy.

"It's gotta go faster and louder," Kathy said. "It's gotta go like this." She hummed out an intense rhythm. "Bammm Bammmm bah-bah-bammmmmm...Think you can do that?"

The drummers looked at each other for a minute, as if they were thinking, "Are we going to take her seriously?" Then one of them counted off the rhythm, clicking his drumsticks. The other guys picked it up, and when they were all playing, the music hit like a boxing glove and kept on hitting. Then Kathy began to sing. And all the feelings from last night—all the anger and hurt and pain—came out in her voice.

When they were through, they were all wet and sweaty. The members of the band looked at each other—they were pleased, Kathy could tell.

"Rock'n' roll!" the drummer with the eye patch finally shouted. Kathy laughed.

"Hey, you're pretty good," said the guitar player with the blond hair. He shook his damp hair off his forehead.

"And you guys can almost keep up with me," Kathy said with a smile.

The band laughed a little.

"You with a band?" asked the drummer.

Kathy shook her head.

"That's good. That's real good," the guitarist said. He was looking at his guitar as he played chords that sounded like punches. "What else do you know?"

Kathy sang with the band for a while. The guys didn't know it, but every song she sang, she sang for Roy.

When she got home that afternoon, Kathy walked around to the back door of the inn to pack up Johnny's tent. A radio was playing somewhere outside, and Kathy followed the music.

Around the side of the garage stood Deena wearing coveralls, rubber gloves, a dust mask, and a kerchief around her hair. She was holding a putty knife in one hand and steel wool in the other. And she was working on the chest—the chest Kathy had been asking her to work on for weeks.

Kathy knew her heart was supposed to throb with

appreciation at this gesture, but it was too little too late.

"If you think you can make things better just by stripping that piece of *junk*, forget it," Kathy sneered.

Deena jumped a little. She hadn't seen Kathy coming. "You scared me," Deena said. It came out muffled because of the mask over her nose and mouth. She removed the gloves and then the mask. "I just started on this because I didn't have anything else scheduled between history and calculus homework. But I've got great news for you."

"What? Someone invented diet junk food?" Kathy said. The sarcasm just automatically kicked in.

"No. I've made up for last night completely," Deena said with confidence. "I talked to your mom about Roy this morning." Her smile was being stretched to its limits. "And I persuaded her to change her mind. You *are* allowed to see him and you *can* go with him to the Bexley Bonfire. Isn't that great?"

"You talked to my mom?! You just don't get it, do you?" Kathy yelled. "You're so smart, but you don't know that one and one are two, not three. What right do *you* have to talk to *my* mom about *my* boyfriend?"

"I was trying to make things better," Deena said, truly bewildered.

"You want to make things better?" Kathy said. "O.K., I'll spell it out for you, so you'll understand. Get out of my life, O.K.? Because I'm sick of you playing with me like I was one of Johnny's little toys. You move me here and tell my mom about the motorcycle. You move me over there and tell me everything's O.K. It's none of your business what goes on in my family. Understand?"

Deena did understand, and she hated to admit it, but Kathy was right.

"Maybe I shouldn't have told about the motorcycle," Deena said. "But *you* really shouldn't have been riding on it."

"Don't tell me what to do!" Kathy exploded. "You think you're so perfect—Miss Athlete, Miss Good Grades, Miss Follow the Crowd and Follow the Rules. It's too much!"

Deena turned around and leaned against the old chest of drawers with her head down. Kathy couldn't see her cousin's face, but she saw small drops of water fall, one by one, onto the dusty top of the chest.

"How do you think it feels to have to be perfect all the time?" Deena said. She turned to face Kathy again. "*Your* mother doesn't expect anything of you—she lets you do whatever you want. But my mother expects me to be organized and responsible. She *expects* me to be perfect. And I get really sick of watching your mother let you ignore the dishes and throw tantrums—while I have to do everything right!"

Kathy shifted uncomfortably on her feet.

"You float in and out of here like a cloud," Deena went on. "And meanwhile I have to do all of the Deena chores and half of the Kathy chores and all my homework. And does your mother ever say anything about it? No! Do you know what my mother would say if *I* had a screaming fit, or slept out in the yard, or did something she told me not to do?"

"I can't help it if your mother's strict," Kathy said.

"I don't want you to help it," Deena said. "I love my mother. I just want you to see what it's like to live with someone who expects me to be perfect!"

Kathy thought about it and she knew Deena was right. Her mom *was* a whole lot easier to deal with than Aunt Lydia. And if she told the truth, Kathy would have to admit that Deena had gotten a raw deal on the chores, too. But was that any reason to *rat* on her and ruin everything with Roy?

No.

But the pizza was.

"Okay. So your mom's a tough nail and my mom's—" Kathy looked around for the right word. "She's just my mom, that's all. I just don't want two mothers—or *three*," she said pointedly. "I'm not trying to change mine—or me. Understand?"

Deena nodded.

"You know last night was a mistake," Deena said. "I hated you for what happened at the Pizza Hut, but I didn't rat on you on purpose. It just slipped out when they were blaming me for everything. I was sorry the minute I said it. Honestly."

"Yeah, I was sorry, too," Kathy said. "I mean, I was sorry about what happened at the Pizza Hut. Zee said she was going to put it on your seat, but I thought she was kidding. We all did. When I saw she'd really done it, I tried to warn you, but it was too late. Zee's a jerk. Anyway, I really am sorry."

"Well, from now on," Deena said, "I'll stay out of things between you and your mom. And if you want me to, I'll stay out of your life completely, too."

"Hey, I didn't mean that," Kathy said quickly, but then she looked away. "Hey—how'd you get my mom to change her mind about Roy?"

Deena smiled and snapped her fingers. "It was easy," she said. "Your mom is the pushover of the Western world. She was already sorry about getting mad at you. Besides, I just told her the truth—that you and I would *never* stop screaming at each other or be friends unless I found some way to make up for tattling on you."

"Yeah, well . . . maybe you are as smart as you think," Kathy said smiling. "Want to hear something funny?"

"Sure."

"I was definitely going to tell my mom about last night with Roy, you know?" Kathy said. "But I also wanted to tell you."

"Really?" Deena asked.

Kathy nodded. "I knew you'd ask me a million questions. Like was he wearing his gloves when he touched my cheeks. Which were the brightest stars? Was he a good kisser? Who stopped kissing first? Was the wind blowing my hair? Did he help me put on the helmet? And on, and on, and I'd get to talk about it the whole night!"

"Wrong, wrong, wrong," Deena said, much to Kathy's surprise. "I'd have asked if he was a good kisser first."

Kathy smiled and felt her face turning red. She picked up a piece of steel wool and began scraping away at the old painted chest. As they worked together, they decided that their mothers still had a lot to learn about running a two-mother-combo family.

After a struggle, they got the third drawer unstuck. And when they opened it, they found a dry but fragile and perfect bird's nest, which they decided to save as a symbol of their new friendship.

* * *

It was finally the night of the Bexley Bonfire. It was a perfect, cold, clear autumn evening, with only a sliver of moon hanging high in the darkening sky. And there was something electric in the air. It was the kind of night, Kathy thought, when you just knew something wonderful was going to happen.

Deena had left early because her committee wanted to get a head start on hanging up the Cranford Fox. The rules were that it had to be placed somewhere public, out in full view. But even side alleys were public, as Ellecia pointed out, and there was a lot of planning and scheming that went into deciding where to put the mascot each year.

Also, the Mascot Committee had to make sure that there were no spies from Bexley following them around when they hung up the fox. So they always drove around for about an hour to be sure they weren't being tailed.

By the time Kathy and Roy got to the bonfire, which

was blazing in a parking lot behind the school, it was almost eight o'clock.

Deena was just getting back from hanging up the fox. And she was about to climb onto the back of a pickup truck full of kids who were going over to Bexley, when a girl tapped her shoulder. Deena looked up and saw a girl she vaguely recognized. She was wearing three layers of pullover sweaters and raggedy jeans. She had a pleasant, kind-of-pretty face, but she wasn't wearing much makeup. And her brown hair was cut short almost everywhere except it dipped a little longer down her neck.

"Hi," the girl said. "We're in Mrs. Godfrey's class together."

Mentally, Deena went over her seating chart. Second row, third seat. Pat Rogus. Her essays always looked great because she used a computer to print them out. "Hi, Pat," Deena said, climbing into the truck. Pat climbed up and sat beside her.

Just then Kathy rode by, behind Roy on his motorcycle.

"Good luck!" Deena called to Kathy, waving her flashlight. "But you'll need it. I've done a psychological profile of the Bexley-ites, and I'm sure *I've* figured out exactly where they put the lion."

"Don't worry," Kathy teased. "Roy and I will show it to you when we bring it back."

Then Roy took off down the road with a roar. They passed Kathy's mom's red van, with Nancy, Lydia, and Johnny inside.

About halfway to Bexley, Roy pointed in front of him and shouted back to Kathy, "Here they come!"

They were like an army. Lines of cars and crowds of kids from Bexley on their way to Cranford.

ROAD CLOSED said the sign on the roadblock just as they got to the rival town.

"We'll have to go another way," Kathy said.

But Roy kicked over the roadblock, saying, "Oldest trick in the book. See? It's just a Bexley High School sign." He showed Kathy the tiny print which identified the sign as belonging to the school, not the police department. Then he climbed back on his motorcycle and started the engine. "Babe, we're closing in," he said as he drove over the roadblock and they zoomed into Bexley.

The next sign they saw said:

WELCOME TO BEXLEY:

A FRIENDLY TOWN.

But someone had added:

UNLESS YOU'RE FROM CRANFORD!

Meanwhile, the truck Deena was in also arrived in Bexley. Soon Deena and Pat were walking through the deserted town.

"You know, I thought your essay on the Eliot poem was fabulous," Pat said.

"Thanks," Deena said.

"Of course, I disagree with it completely, but it was really well done," Pat said. "Do you see the lion yet?"

"No," Deena said. For a second she even forgot what

she was looking for. "Why did you disagree with my essay?"

"Bexley certainly isn't Cranford, is it?" Pat said. "Lousy bookstore. Only best sellers."

"I think they must be low lifes," Deena said. "They have a fourteen-theater cineplex here! Was it my premise or my conclusions you disagreed with?"

"Oh, let's forget it. I refuse to talk about school work tonight," Pat said, even though she was the one who brought it up.

While Deena and Pat were searching the village, Kathy was sitting on a parked motorcycle on the outskirts of Bexley. It was only nine o'clock, and she and Roy had looked nearly everywhere already.

"If I were a papier-mâché lion, where would I be?" Roy said.

"In a lot of trouble if it rained," Kathy said with a laugh. "Or maybe you'd be in your papier-mâché den."

Roy looked at her for a second and then yelled, "Way to go, Babe!"

He kick-started the cycle.

"Where are we going?" Kathy asked.

"To Denny Road," Roy said. "I forgot all about it."

When they got to Denny Road, they found a quiet, dark neighborhood of large houses that ended in a cul-de-sac. In the middle of the cul-de-sac there was a flag-pole. And on top of the flagpole was the Bexley Lion.

Unfortunately, there were also five enormous Bexley football players standing around the flagpole like guards.

"That's cheating, isn't it?" Kathy asked Roy.

"Yeah," Roy said. "This isn't going to be easy."

"I don't think they've seen us," Kathy whispered to Roy. Then she whispered an idea in his ear.

A minute later Kathy hopped off the bike and walked into someone's front yard. Roy shut off the motor and walked his cycle away. Then Kathy started singing, full-volume, vintage Nuclear Waste. The five guys looked at each other and then started to follow Kathy's voice. As soon as they were far enough away from the flagpole, Kathy heard Roy start his cycle. He rode up, climbed the pole, cut the lion loose, and hopped back on the bike with it before the five guys could get back to stop him. Then Roy zoomed back to pick up Kathy, who was hiding behind a large tree.

"You know what I'd like to do?" Roy shouted as they rode away. "Hide this thing in my garage. Everyone in Cranford would go nuts looking for it!"

Kathy burst out laughing at the idea. "That would be a riot," she said. "But let's not. It would drive Deena *too* crazy."

They drove through Bexley, shouting, "We've got it! We found it!" so that everyone would know to go back to Cranford.

The ride back to Cranford was fantastic. Roy was in front, of course, laughing the whole time. And the captured Bexley Lion was strapped on the handlebars in front of him. Every time they passed someone from Cranford, the car would honk to congratulate Roy and Kathy for finding the mascot first.

When they got to the bonfire back home, the high

school band played and the crowd cheered. Roy waved the lion over his head for everyone to see, and the crowd yelled even louder. Then he handed it to Kathy. "I said I couldn't find it without you," he said. "You burn it!"

The crowd began chanting. "Burn the lion!" Kathy hugged Roy and then started to walk toward the blazing bonfire to throw the Bexley Lion in.

But at the last minute she stopped and looked around her. There were people everywhere—some of them people she was beginning to know. She saw Mr. Millander, and A.J., and even Mrs. Godfrey. Then she saw her mother and her aunt, and there was Johnny yelling "Touchdown!" because he was moving into football season. Kathy looked at every face until finally she saw the one she was looking for. There was Deena. Kathy dashed through the crowd and grabbed her cousin's arm.

"Come on," Kathy said, pulling Deena with her.

"I don't know if I can burn it," Deena said, admiring the Bexley Lion. "It must have been so much work!"

"Big deal," Kathy said, smiling. "Let's do it!"

"Burn the lion!" the crowd chanted. And then some guy called out, "Come on, let's do it! Throw it in, Cranberry Cousins!"

And for the first time, hearing those two words together made both girls smile. No one was taking sides. Everyone was cheering for them both.

Together Kathy and Deena lifted the papier-mâché lion above their heads and heaved it into the fire. And the crowd went wild.